Invincible Voices
Winter Shorts

Books by Zoe Antoniades

Invincible Voices: Short Shorts
Invincible Voices: Medium Shorts
Invincible Voices: Long Shorts

Invincible Voices
Winter Shorts

Zoe Antoniades

Front cover illustration by Athena Estrada

Matador
9 Priory Business Park,
Wistow Road, Kibworth Beauchamp,
Leicestershire. LE8 0RX
Tel: 0116 279 2299
Email: books@troubador.co.uk
Web: www.troubador.co.uk/matador
Twitter: @matadorbooks

ISBN 978 1789014 334

British Library Cataloguing in Publication Data.
A catalogue record for this book is available from the British Library.

Printed and bound by CPI Group (UK) Ltd, Croydon, CR0 4YY
Typeset in 12pt Aldine401 BT by Troubador Publishing Ltd, Leicester, UK

Matador is an imprint of Troubador Publishing Ltd

Zoe Antoniades was born in West London in 1973. She graduated from the University of Hull with a degree in English and Drama and later trained as a teacher at the Institute of Education.

Her Invincible Voices company provides creative writing workshops for young people where the stories in this publication have been brought to life. The first three anthologies of short stories in the Invincible Voices series, *Short Shorts*, *Medium Shorts* and *Long Shorts,* were launched in 2017.

Zoe has also written a memoir, *Tea and Baklavas* which won the Winchester Writers' Festival Memoir Prize and is published in Winchester University's *Best of 2015*.

www.zoeantoniades.com

Little voices made big

These stories are *for* children *by* children; they contain first-hand concepts that children want to read about because children have chosen to write them. With a skilled teacher and author, Zoe Antoniades, to guide them, the children are inspired to come up with their own ideas, then helped to shape, structure, organise and develop them so that they evolve into more professional pieces. The result of such an approach is a unique style, a hybrid product of adult and child's voice. The stories possess the spirit and originality of a child's creative ideas, but with the polish and flair of an experienced writer.

Invincible Authors

Zoe Antoniades
Simran Ahuja
Tejas Akavarapu
Hasnain Alibhai
Parampreet Amole
Ashpriya Baryan
Harjeet Baryan
Sam Beglin
Amira Bukhari
Daniela Burger
Matthew Burger
Louise Chassard
Saranya Chatterjee
Mattheus Daly
Janasi Damania
Eshani De Silva
Keyshia Edomioya
Alexander Eric-Kovacevic
Alexia Estrada
Athena Estrada

Despina Estrada
Abdifatah Farhan
Aaryan Ghag
Cara Gulzar
Chahat Gupta Chaudhary
Adam Hakiem
Sumedha Hazari
Mahad Kokhar
Zakir Ladha
Darcey McKeever
Maya Nampoothiri
Vayu Oberoi
Anusha Ruj
Siddhant Shetty
Anisha Sinha
Adeline Veschi
Calista Veschi
Adhiraj Warik
Pavan Yadlapati
Sai Yadlapati
Jessica Yu

Contents

Prologue

By Jessica Yu

The wonderful season of winter has arrived with its glistening, glimmering, deep-pile carpets of pearl-white snow. Children revelling in the building of silvery snowmen with carrot noses and eyes of coal, engaging in snowball battles, firing while the enemy's back is turned, skating on firm, translucent ice in the chill of the dusky air, sledging downhill and tumbling into a freezing fluff-pile. Just messing about in the snow - it's so delightful.

Merriest is Christmas, a time for family and friends to share. The anticipation on Christmas Eve, then waking up to the sight of stockings full of sweets, toys and books galore - it's simply marvellous. Rushing to the tree, seeking out the presents and scuffling to find the one that's yours - tearing it open to discover your heart's desire - just what you've always wanted. Then leaping about for joy. Fantastic. That's what Christmas is. Just fantastic.

After the hustle, the bustle, the overexcitement and thrills, the year draws to a close. Feeling thankful, yet sentimental, as it will soon be gone forever. Hopeful still, as another is just around the corner. Ready for new dreams to begin.

Christmas Chaos

By Adeline, Alexia, Amira, Anisha, Athena, Cara,
Despina, Jessica and Parampreet

Monday 8th December

Dear Diary

Everyone usually hates Mondays, but today was different. At school, during registration, Mrs Broomfield announced that this year, it would be our class' turn to put on the Nativity performance. Some of us, of course, were ecstatic whilst others plunged into despair. I was somewhere in the middle. It would obviously mean more homework - all those lines and songs to learn.

Not that I'll get a much of a role anyway. I never get a main part - hardly ever even a speaking part actually. Last year, when we did Little Red Riding Hood, I had to be a tree. I mean, a tree! But this time, maybe, just

maybe, I could get to be the show's star. *The* Star! You know, as in the one that leads the shepherds, the wise men and everyone to the Baby Jesus. It's been my dream, ever since nursery, to be the star. Maybe, just maybe, this year will be my chance to shine. Shine - ha, ha - get it? The auditions are tomorrow, so we'll have to wait and see.

Tuesday 9th December

Dear Diary

You'll never believe what happened! It was sooooo frustrating!!!

So, today we had the auditions. Anyone who'd signed up for them had to have an early lunch (bonus!) and be at the music and drama room by 12.30.

There was a long line of children all waiting in

the corridor for Mrs Broomfield to let us in. Marcus turned up, worse luck! (I can't stand Marcus. Name any bad thing you want, Marcus has done it - except the teachers never see, he's sneaky like that, they all think he's marvellous, for some unknown reason). He barged his way to the front of the line - soooo annoying! But of course when the teachers came out, he acted all goody-two-shoes.

Mrs Broomfield was with Mr Parkinson (our headmaster) and the head girl and head boy were there too. They really were taking the judging seriously this year! We all had to sit down on the carpet and wait to be called to the front to read from a page of script.

Helen and Amar got up and tried out for Mary and Joseph. They weren't bad, but I knew my best friend Alex could do better. She was up next with Craig. Craig was a bit drippy but still, he didn't cramp Alex's style. She was brilliant. She had the clearest, loudest voice and everything. I could see the judges all nodding to one another as they made their notes. Fingers crossed, Alex gets the part.

I sat there, with butterflies in my stomach, waiting for them to get to the auditions for the Star-of-Wonder. It took ages. It seemed they were auditioning every single part except the one I wanted. After Mary and Joseph, they did the Wise Men, then the Angel Gabriel, then the shepherds and even the old donkey!

There was a further delay when Wimpy William got up to try out for a solo. He stood there for an eternity. The teachers were being all patient and encouraging, but the whole time I was just screaming inside my head, "Get on with it!" Why on earth would he audition if it was such torture for him? His mum must have made him or something.

Marcus started to snigger. He did it behind my back so it looked like it was me who was laughing. He's always trying to get people into trouble like that. The teachers didn't notice Marcus, of course. But William did, and he burst into tears. Marcus muttered under his breath, "Such a cry-baby," as William scurried off. The teachers didn't notice *that* either.

Finally it was time for the Star-of-Wonder. Anyone who wanted to try out for the part had to sing a solo. Marcus elbowed me out of the way, so I had to wait even longer. I was willing him to sing out of tune or for all the words to come out wrong, but much as I hate to admit it, he was actually really good. When he finished, all the judges spontaneously got to their feet and applauded. A standing ovation! I mean, he was good, but not *that* good.

By the time it got to be my turn, lunch break was almost over and I could tell the teachers were keen to wrap things up and get everyone back to class. They were practically already tidying away their papers as I took my position. I wanted the part so badly. I'd even worn my gold sparkly headband especially for the occasion. But they hardly even looked at me. And *then*, when I was singing, Marcus started having a coughing fit. I wasn't fooled. I knew he was doing it on purpose because he kept eyeballing me the whole time. He totally ruined everything!

Wednesday 10th December

Dear Diary

So, today Mrs Broomfield announced our parts. Guess what? I'm the donkey. Not only that, I'm the back end of the donkey! Really, I haven't got over the shock yet. Worse still, Marcus got to be the star. I mean, how is anyone meant to gaze up at *him* in awe!? At least my best friend Alex got a decent part. She's Mary. I'm happy for her, anyway.

Thursday 11th December

Dear Diary

Today we began rehearsals for the Nativity. The donkey costume is gross. It smells like it's been in an actual barn, under a pile of manure. The real truth behind the rotten smell is even worse. It's stale vomit, from when the boy who was playing the part last year threw up in it. Miss Morgan our TA insisted that she'd washed it thoroughly, but I could still smell the rankness of it. It made me want to puke, myself.

Anyway, I did my bit and followed Mrs Broomfield's directions. I managed to get Mary and Joseph to Bethlehem as instructed (which wasn't easy, as being the back end of the donkey, you can't exactly see that much).

It wasn't until we were halfway through the play and the Baby Jesus was meant to have been born, when Mrs Broomfield realised we didn't *actually* have a baby to be Jesus himself.

Jerbert, one of the Wise Men, piped up with a not-so-wise suggestion, "We could get one of the little kids from nursery to be it."

"I think we might need a prop, like a doll, rather than a real child," explained Mrs Broomfield. "We don't want someone clambering out of the manger halfway through the play and crying out for his mummy."

Toby raised his hand, "I've got a doll at home!" Everyone turned and stared at him, then burst out laughing. Toby went bright red, "It's not mine!" he said in frustration, "It's Becky's. I'll bring it in tomorrow."

Everyone knows who 'adorable' little Becky is.

She's Toby's two-year-old sister. Have you heard of the terrible twos? Well that's Becky. Every morning she toddles into school when Toby is being dropped off, wailing for him to come to play group with her instead.

The best thing about today was that Marcus was off school with a cold. Serves him right for having a fake coughing fit all over my audition. Looks like he's got one for real now. A whole Marcus-free day. Heaven!

Anyway, I still have to do my homework, so I'll catch up with you some more tomorrow.

Friday 12th December

Dear Diary

Best news ever! Marcus' cough turned into laryngitis. He's completely lost his voice. Even better still, Mrs Broomfield has given his part to *me*. I get to be the Star-of-Wonder after all. AND, you're never going to believe this, Marcus has to swap with me and now *he's* the back end of the stinky donkey. I could tell he was really fuming about it because he kept going in the wrong direction and falling over. Everyone was laughing at him. That'll teach him for sniggering at us behind the teachers' backs all the time. Even Mrs Broomfield got annoyed with him and kept telling him to make more of an effort. Not so perfect now, eh! Finally the teachers are beginning to see his true colours.

Toby brought Becky's doll in today to be the baby Jesus. It's got masses of bright, ginger hair. I'm not sure Jesus was a red-head or that babies have that much hair when they're born, but Miss Morgan seemed happy enough with it and put the doll with all the other props she's been busily sorting out.

She's in charge of our costumes as well. She's got them all organised on a rail at the back of our classroom. I think she's done a great job. I love mine. It's a sparkly gold robe that goes right down to the floor. Miss Morgan says I can wear my headband too (the one I had on at the audition). She's going to attach some gold triangles to it to make it look more starry. It's going to be great.

Sabrina was less satisfied with her costume. She's one of the angels and is insisting on wearing pink. I mean, who ever heard of a pink angel?! A fairy maybe, but this is a Nativity not a pantomime. Hopefully Miss Morgan can get her to see sense by next week, because we've only got one more rehearsal left and the actual play is on Tuesday.

Can't wait!

Monday 14th December

Dear Diary

Sorry I didn't write anything over the weekend. We went to visit Aunt Pat and Uncle Jim in Sussex for a pre-Christmas family get together, and I forgot to bring you with me.

Anyway, back to today. This was our last day of rehearsals before the big performance - which is tomorrow! Mrs Broomfield and Miss Morgan were stressed out, trying to pull it all together, so we spent the ENTIRE day practising. Jerbert, Craig and Amar drove Mrs Broomfield spare as they kept forgetting their lines. It was hilarious when she yelled at them, "You're meant to be *wise* men not absent-minded men!" Then, she almost lost it completely when Jerbert presented the Baby Jesus with Frankenstein. "It's frankincense, Jerbert, how many times!" she despaired.

Anyway, it'll be alright on the night, as they say in showbiz. Hopefully…

Tuesday 15th December

Dear Diary

Today has to go down in history as one of the most unforgettable days of my life, and I'm glad I've got you, Diary, to look after my memories.

As you know, it was our big performance today. We all got into our costumes (Sabrina managed to be the first pink angel of all time - Miss Morgan gave up in the end) and took our positions back stage. Peeping through a gap in the side-curtain, I could see the hall bursting with parents. I was a bundle of nerves and excitement. Mostly, I couldn't wait to get on that stage.

Mr Parkinson did a welcome speech and reminded everyone to put their mobile phones on silent, and then it was time for the play to begin.

Everything was going quite well until Marcus, the reluctant donkey, plodded on. He'd been in a permanent sulk since having to swap parts with me and he still hadn't taken on Mrs Broomfield's directions. He ended up going the wrong way. He messed up so badly that the donkey split in two. The front end fell off the stage, whilst Marcus, the back end, crash-landed into the row of angels, toppling them like dominoes.

Things just went from bad to worse after that. Jerbert proudly presented the Baby Jesus with his

gift of 'Frankenstein' causing Mrs Broomfield to yelp so loudly backstage, the entire audience must have heard it. It didn't however, stop Jerbert's mother from standing up, full of pride and shouting out, "That's my boy!" across the hall.

When it was time to sing, 'Away in a Manger,' Mary (my friend, Alex) had to pick up the Baby Jesus and rock him in her arms. Several people in the audience chuckled when his shock of red hair was revealed. That was also the moment when Toby's little sister, Becky, recognised her toy doll.

"That's mine!" she screamed, tearing herself away from her mum who had been helplessly trying to restrain her. Becky bolted across the audience, clambered onto the stage, fought her way through the wise men, the

shepherds, the cattle and the angels and snatched the doll back from Alex.

All the mums and dads in the audience were laughing their heads off. The entire cast was rolling around on the stage, everyone all in the wrong places, with the backdrop falling down, wonky-winged angels with crooked halos, wise men tumbling headfirst into the manger, shepherds chasing after their stray sheep… it was pandemonium!

But the thing that bothered me was, we still hadn't got to the part where I was meant to sing my solo. I was determined to have my moment. The play might have descended into chaos but nothing was going to stop me. I caught Miss Morgan's eye and signalled her to turn the music on.

I stepped forwards, clutched my hands to my chest, held my head high and began to sing…

Star of wonder, star of night
Star with royal beauty bright
Westward leading, still proceeding
Guide us to thy perfect light

And, as if by magic, things calmed down. All eyes looked to me as everyone listened. Mrs Broomfield and Miss Morgan smiled at one another, the audience sat back in their seats, Becky climbed onto Mary's (Alex's) lap and cuddled her 'Jesus' doll, the toppled angels got to their feet and straightened their halos, the sheep snuggled up to their shepherds, the three not-so-wise men managed to look a little less all over the place - even the donkey somehow pulled itself back together.

And all the while, I kept on singing. I sang my heart out. When it came round to the second chorus, everyone joined in, including the mums and dads.

And guess what! As we all sang together, the first snowflake in four years, came drifting down from the sky. It was truly something special.

So thanks, Diary, for being here to hold onto these memories for me. Keep them safe now.

Night night!

The Crystal Compass

By Adam, Alex, Alexia, Athena, Chahat, Darcey, Despina, Jessica and Parampreet

Legend had it that on top of Norway's highest mountain, a cold-hearted Snow Beast stood guard of a Never-Melting Icicle. Many had journeyed in search of it, but no-one had ever returned to tell the tale.

One such adventurer had been Francis Almanov, the father of a young lad named Noah. Noah was just three years old when his father had set off on his quest to seek out the Never-Melting Icicle. His father was a distant memory now, but Noah's determination to be reunited with him when he grew up never faded.

Now it was his eighteenth birthday, the day he had been waiting for all these years. It was also the day his mother had been dreading, for she knew she would have to let her son go.

"Blow out your candles, Son. Make a wish," she whispered, holding back her tears as she presented Noah with his cake.

It was just the two of them. No big party. They were poor. Ever since they had lost Noah's father, it had been a struggle to get by, and so they lived humbly in their tiny, ramshackle cottage.

There was no need to guess what Noah's wish would be. To find his father. His mother longed for him to return unharmed. This was of course unheard of, yet she had something that provided her with the tiniest hope.

It was the birthday gift which she had bought for Noah from the old second-hand shop at the end of the lane. The shop mostly sold old junk, but earlier that week, when Noah's mother had sifted through the worn-out trinkets in search of a present for her son's eighteenth birthday, something had caught her eye. It glinted at her from the corner of the topmost shelf. The shopkeeper noticed her looking up at it.

"Ah, that'll be the crystal compass. Not a bad little knick-knack, that. Would you like to have a proper look at it?"

"If you don't mind," Noah's mother had replied.

The shopkeeper fetched a wooden step-ladder and climbed up to retrieve the object for her. It was covered in dust and one of its corners was slightly cracked, but on closer inspection, Noah's mother could see that the face of the compass had the most intricate design. It really was quite special. She polished it with her scarf and the crystal compass seemed almost to glow. She hoped the shopkeeper wouldn't want too much for it.

"No, don't worry. You can have it for a few coins if you like. To be honest, it's been up there on that shelf for so long, I'd almost forgotten about it. No one's shown any interest in it up until now. So take it with my blessing. And I hope your lad has a happy birthday and a bright and prosperous future."

Noah's mother couldn't believe her luck. There was something about that compass and she was certain her son would like it.

So after Noah blew out his birthday candles, his mother handed him his special gift.

"It's for your travels," she said, forcing a smile. "Can't have you getting lost now, can we?"

Noah marvelled at the crystal compass. Turning it between his fingers it began to glow again, just as it had done back in the old second-hand shop. He too could tell there was something special about it.

Noah noticed a tear slipping down his mother's cheek.

"I think I'll go and pack my things now," he said, turning away, for he couldn't bear to see his mother upset.

As he got his belongings together, he wondered whether he would make it home with his father or suffer the same fate of all those other explorers and simply disappear, never to return.

The time to leave had come. The moment Noah's mother had been dreading. Saying goodbye to her son, tore at her heart. She stood at the door waving him off. "Be safe," she wept as she watched him trail away, hoping against hope that the compass would protect him.

Noah consulted his guidebook. The Polar Bear Express was due to arrive at any moment. There came a clattering from the clouds above, through

which burst a line of a dozen bears of the purest white, harnessed together with silver reins. They arrived with a flourish on a trail of snowflakes, coming to land just short of Noah's boots.

"Welcome to the Polar Bear Express," hailed the bear at the front of the train.

Crunching through the snow, Noah stepped up to the train. He noticed that each bear wore a red saddle made of plush velvet with silver stitching. He climbed on and taking hold of the reins in one hand and clutching his crystal compass in the other, Noah braced himself for take-off.

Before he knew it, he was flying high in the sky. The clouds were like stretched cotton wool and

Noah was tempted to grab one for comfort. But he was eighteen now and he could be brave.

Eventually the train descended onto a cold mountainous terrain and came to a stop.

"You have reached your destination," proclaimed the head bear. "Please dismount the Polar Bear Express."

Noah smiled to himself. He was one step closer to finding his father. He jumped off the polar bear's back and watched the train soar off up into the sky and out of sight.

Noah looked all around. He felt as if he was in the middle of nowhere. He felt alone.

Noah's guidebook told him that the Never-Melting Icicle was said to be in a cave at the heart of Mount Colossus. But there were so many mountains in that cold, desolate land, Noah had no clue as to which one it was.

He took out his crystal compass and examined

its face more closely. The arrow gleamed and whizzed around until it aligned itself with the tallest mountain of all.

Sparked with renewed confidence, Noah allowed the compass to guide him towards the mountain. The closer he got, the colder the air became. Snow began to fall, and the closer he trudged towards the mountain, the more harshly it came down. Blown by a cruel wind, it stung his face and numbed his fingers. He could barely keep grip of the compass.

Now Noah was at the foot of the mountain. It loomed largely, overpowering him in its great, dark shadow. Yet the compass reassuringly glowed in Noah's palm. Its radiance stronger than ever. He must be close now.

The compass pointed towards a deep, jagged fracture in the mountain. Noah slipped through into the darkness. He reached for his torch, but soon realised he didn't need it, for the compass now glowed with an extreme luminosity that lit up the inside of the mountain. Noah stood at the top of a long tunnel which led downwards, deep into the heart of the mountain.

He followed the trail which seemed to go on forever. He hadn't known what to expect on reaching the end, but the scene that met him when he did, was beyond anything he could have imagined.

He found himself at the edge of a vast cave, its ceiling festooned with blue icicles that dripped methodically into a lake below. At the centre of this lake stood a plinth of brilliant white snow, at the top of which prevailed the Never-Melting Icicle - a tall, majestic, translucent spire that stood regally, with an aura of great importance. Noah, transfixed by its magnificence, found himself drawn towards it.

On stepping forwards, there came the sound of gentle hoof-beats. From the darkness of the mountain emerged a beautiful, white reindeer with silver antlers. The noble creature peacefully circled the Never-Melting Icicle.

Was this the monstrous Snow Beast that everyone talked of? Surely such an innocent looking creature couldn't be the cause of the disappearance of so many explorers, his father included. Noah wondered where this so-called Snow Beast indeed kept his victims. He decided to approach the snowy reindeer to see if he could find out.

Inching closer, he reached out his hand to pat the reindeer's exquisite fur. But as he did so, the beautiful creature immediately transformed into the most hideous being. He expanded to an enormous size. He broke out in icy spikes and frosty scales and developed great, sharp teeth. His antlers transformed into giant, jagged horns and he grew the wings of a dragon. The Snow Beast towered over Noah, fearsome and formidable.

"Who dares to enter my realm and disturb the Never-Melting Icicle!" he roared menacingly.

"If… if… if you please, Your Gracious Beastness, I… I… I don't mean any harm…" stammered Noah.

But the Snow Beast hollered back in disbelief, "Just visiting were you? Never, in all the years I have reigned, has anyone come for any other reason. Trespasser, you must pay, just as everyone else has done before you!"

With that, the Snow Beast flared his great nostrils, and blasted Noah with a furious blizzard. Noah believed this was surely to be his end, yet the strangest, most unexpected thing happened.

The compass lit up. It glowed more brilliantly

than it had ever done before and from the top of it, shot a giant translucent beam of light, which encircled Noah to form a dome-shaped protective shield around him.

The blizzard was repelled by the compass' defences and the Snow Beast could only look on in bewilderment. Stunned by this vision, the Snow Beast calmed his fury and ceased his stormy attack.

Noah too, was astonished by the power of the compass. Under its protection, Noah felt inspired to try to negotiate with the Snow Beast once more.

"If you please, I truly have not come for the Never-Melting Icicle. My only wish is to be reunited with my father…" and then a heavy tear rolled down his cheek. "I haven't seen him since I was a small child. In all these years, I've never stopped thinking about him. It feels as if my life is an unfinished jigsaw puzzle. It's the same for my mother too. She tries so hard to be strong, but all too often I hear her sobbing at night."

The Snow Beast's heart began to melt and he gradually reduced in size. His wings disappeared, his horns reverted to silver antlers, the spikes retreated and the scales transformed back into a beautiful, snowy fur coat - the hideous Snow Beast had returned to his peaceful reindeer state.

"It's alright," the majestic reindeer replied, "I believe your story. Your father is safe. As are all the others. Yet I keep them here for good reason.

It is my duty to protect the Never-Melting Icicle. It must remain intact. To disturb it would mean the end of the world. Earth would perish in a giant apocalyptic storm."

"So… you mean… my father… is… is alive?"

"Indeed he is. I have kept your father and all the others safe. It is not my intention to destroy anyone or anything. It is you humans who are the destructive ones."

"But now that we know the importance of the Never-Melting Icicle, we will certainly leave it alone. If you could just return my father and the others I promise that no one will ever disturb you again."

"I believe this to be true of you, but you cannot speak for all of mankind. Whilst the Never-Melting Icicle exists, people will always come for it."

"But… but… you can't…"

"I haven't finished. I have a proposal. Call it a trade-off. I will return your father to you, in exchange for the compass you have in your possession. Its mystical powers will be of great use here. The protective shield can keep the Never-Melting Icicle from harm."

Noah understood, and without delay, placed the compass on the plinth beside the Never-Melting Icicle. Both the icicle and the reindeer became encased in its protective dome. The reindeer trotted gently over to the compass and inspected it closely. He gave it a nudge and the cave began to shudder and shake. The icicles trembled at the roof of the cave, ripples ran through the lake, and a vast sheet of ice, which formed the back wall of the cave, cracked. The crevice widened and a brilliant white glow came from what must have been a further cave beyond the ice wall. As Noah adjusted his eyes to the glare, he watched as shadowy figures emerged from the light and staggered towards him.

Noah rushed towards the crowd of tired-looking men, all wrapped in furs. He searched feverishly for his father amongst them. And there he was. Although he hadn't seen him in fifteen years, Noah knew him at once. Francis Almanov. Noah gripped his father's arms and looked intently into his eyes.

"Father. It's me. Noah. I've come to take you home."

And the two of them, father and son, fell onto one another in a deep embrace. Noah, who had lost his father as a boy, had become the man to have found him. It was a reunion that time would never forget.

Aluki

By Matthew Burger

Aluki was a young boy who lived in an igloo in the arctic regions of Canada. He loved to read, especially legends. His favourite, was about an arctic seal which was said to talk at the stroke of midnight, on Christmas Eve. Aluki strongly believed in that legend and he was desperate to see the special arctic seal with his own eyes.

Christmas was fast approaching and Aluki found himself waking up on the morning of Christmas Eve exploding with excitement. Leaping from his bed of fur, to the breakfast table, he asked his dad, "Can I use your boat today?"

"What for?" replied Dad suspiciously.

"Erm… to fish…?" said Aluki looking up at the ceiling.

"You're not wanting to go after that talking seal again, are you? Come on now, Son, we have this nonsense every year," sighed Dad.

"But…"

"I don't want to hear another word on the subject. You're not taking the boat and that's that," concluded Dad.

But Aluki was determined.

He patiently waited until it was time to go in search of the legendary seal. He shoved some food in his bag, crept around to the back of the igloo, untied the boat and rowed away.

Aluki kept track of the time as he feasted on a fish eye, "Five minutes to twelve, four minutes to

twelve, three minutes, two, one…" Aluki counted down with excitement.

Whilst searching around for the talking Arctic seal, he leaned too far over the edge of the boat, not realising that he was dangerously weighing down the side.

The boat capsized, throwing Aluki and all of his belongings into the cold icy sea. Worse still, the oars were nowhere to be seen. Using all his determination and pushing ever so hard against the underside of the boat, he managed to turn it the right way up.

Suddenly, without any warning, a seal came shooting out of the sea and landed in the boat. He had Aluki's bag around his neck.

Aluki was speechless, "Are you...?" he just about managed to mutter before fainting.

When Aluki came to his senses, he found his boat was moving along by itself. Even with the oars gone. It was the seal! He was nudging the boat all the way to the shore.

Aluki decided to ask his saviour a question to see if he was indeed the famous talking seal.

"What's your name?" he ventured.

The seal replied, "Archy."

"Wow," replied Aluki, amazed to find that the seal could indeed talk. "My name's Aluki."

"It's nice to meet you," nodded the seal.

"Pleasure to meet you too. And thanks so much for helping me."

As the boat approached home, Aluki knew his adventure was coming to an end.

"Will I ever see you again?" he asked.

Archy replied, "You never know!" And with that, the mysterious seal slid back into the water and swam away.

Aluki waved farewell, turned towards home and walked thoughtfully along the snow, back to his igloo. Everyone was asleep, so he tiptoed quietly to his bed and lay down reflecting on the amazing experience he'd had. He wouldn't tell anyone about

Archy. Humans would only want to take over. Archy deserved to be left alone, wild and free.

From that day on, Aluki returned to the spot where he had once met Archy, but years went by with no sign of him. Every time Aluki rowed his boat out, he would stop and call, "Archy, Archy, if you're out there somewhere, I just want you to know that I miss you lots and I'll never forget you."

Robin

By Adhiraj, Chahat, Eshani, Maya, Saranya, Siddhant and Vayu

It was a cosy winter's evening, and Kate and her mother were getting supper ready in the kitchen. As Kate set the table, she gazed out onto their beautiful back garden. A layer of frost covered the vast lawn which glistened under the moonlight. A path wound its way towards an ornamental fountain; no water flowed from it though, for it always froze in the winter. Kate felt it a shame as she always enjoyed watching the birds bathing there during the warmer seasons.

There came the rattle of a key in the door. Kate knew it was Dad arriving home from work.

"Daddy!" cheered Kate, noticing he was hiding something behind his back.

"Surprise!" he smiled, pulling out a strange cage-like contraption, shaped like a cylinder, and a box of balls that looked like spherical flapjacks.

"What's that, Daddy?" Kate asked.

"It's a bird feeder," explained Dad, "and these are seed balls to go inside it."

"Oh, Daddy, that's what I've always wished for," said Kate, throwing her arms around him.

"That'll definitely come in handy with everything so frozen out there," said Mum, coming over to have a look. "The poor birds can hardly peck at the ground now, can they?"

"It's your responsibility to look after it," said Dad.

"Can we put it up now, Daddy?" asked Kate eagerly.

"Let's have supper first," suggested Mum.

Kate ate her dinner in a flash and kept urging her parents to hurry up. At last, it was time to hang the bird feeder up outside. Kate carefully filled it with the seed balls, then they went out into the moonlit garden and hung it up on a tall, ancient oak tree.

The sound of tweeting caught Kate's attention. She looked up to notice a little robin perched on the washing line. Its upper feathers were brown and it had a whitish belly, but its iconic feature was of course its blazing red breast. It tilted its head and blinked its eyes at her. Then it chirruped again.

"I think it's trying to say thank you," chuckled Kate.

"Don't be silly," scoffed Dad. "Robins can't talk."

"But look at the way it's staring at us. I really do believe it understands," insisted Kate.

"Maybe," replied Mum, "but right now, it's late, and you've got school tomorrow. You really need to get to bed."

"But can't we just stay for a little while longer to watch the birds feeding?" pleaded Kate.

"The birds need their sleep, just like you. Let's look out for them tomorrow morning at breakfast," replied Mum.

With that, they all went back inside. The robin tweeted once more.

"See, Daddy. The robin's saying goodnight," said Kate.

"Whatever you say, sweetheart," replied Dad, shaking his head in disbelief.

The next morning, Kate dashed down to the kitchen to join her parents, but it wasn't *her* breakfast she was interested in, it was the birds'. They flitted to and from the feeder, as if taking turns. The robin seemed to really enjoy pecking at the nuts and seeds and when it had finished, it flew up to the window sill, tilted its head and chirruped as if to say, "What a delightful breakfast."

"Look! The bird feeder really works," said Kate clapping her hands in delight. She and the robin were certainly becoming the best of friends.

However, at that moment, the clouds thickened and the sky darkened. The oak tree shuddered and shivered, and from out of it appeared a brown, bushy-tailed squirrel. It leapt like lightning onto the bird feeder, and clung on upside down with its strong, sharp claws. It gnawed and nibbled at the tasty treats, chewing away until its belly was completely full.

"Look! That cheeky, greedy squirrel has gobbled up the lot! There's nothing left for the birds," gasped Kate.

The robin dipped its head and gave one single melancholy peep.

"Even the robin's upset," Kate sighed. "What are we going to do?"

"Tell you what," said Dad brightly, "I'll hang it on the washing line. That squirrel will have no chance of getting up there."

Kate and Mum thought it was a great idea. They watched from the window as Dad untied the bird feeder from the oak tree, refilled it with treats and hung it from the long, thin washing line which stretched across the lawn.

Kate thrust her hands in the air triumphantly and the robin hopped up and down on the window sill.

"See, the robin thinks it's an excellent idea as well," agreed Mum.

"Don't you go thinking that the robin speaks our language too," said Dad, shaking his head.

However, the next day, when Kate and her parents observed the birdfeeder with anticipation, it wasn't a flurry of feathered friends that came to visit. It was the naughty squirrel again, who, like some sort of acrobat, was not giving up. It twitched

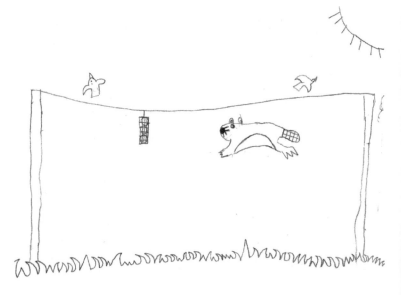

its nose and sniffed the air. Its eyes shone with mischief and hunger.

It marched up to the washing line, scaled the pole and skilfully balanced on the wire, as if it were a trained tightrope walker, then zipped along the line towards the bird feeder.

Kate and her family could not believe their eyes as they watched the squirrel hang upside down by its tail, just like a monkey might do, and stretch itself like elastic to reach its prize. It chipped away at the bird food and within minutes it had completely emptied the feeder again. It even managed to knock a whole seed ball out onto the ground. The rascally squirrel bounded down to retrieve it and clutching the seed ball in its razor sharp claws, it scampered away back to its hideout to stash its treasure.

"Whatever are we to do about that naughty, greedy squirrel?" cried Kate.

There was a long silence as everyone had a good think.

"How about putting an alarm on the bird feeder so that every time the squirrel pounces, it beeps?" suggested Mum.

"But it will be beeping all the time, even when the birds are on it. And all that noise will startle the birds themselves too," explained Dad.

Mum had another idea, "What about if we set up a decoy, to deter the squirrel?"

"What, like a scarecrow, you mean?" said Dad.

"But that will just frighten the birds away as well," sighed Kate.

Dad scratched his head, then piped up, "We could set up a CCTV camera."

That idea was so extreme, both Mum and Kate burst out laughing all at once.

"We're not the FBI, you know," chuckled Mum.

The robin broke into chirrups as if it were joining in with the laughter too.

"I've got it!" cried Kate. "That clever robin understands everything. I'm just going to feed it from its own special dish here on the window sill. It can take its meals with us whenever we eat. That squirrel wouldn't dare to be so bold as to come near its supper when we're all here watching too."

"Come on now, Kate. The robin's a wild bird, it won't come that near," said Dad, shaking his head.

"Just let her give it a try," urged Mum.

And so, Kate took a small plastic bowl and crumbled one of the seed balls into it. She then lifted up the sash window and carefully placed the bowl on the sill. The robin tilted its head, then hopped towards it as if inspecting its feast. It dipped its beak and pecked at the seeds, then looked up at Kate and ruffled its feathers.

"I think it's trying to say, 'That was delicious,'" said Kate, speaking on the robin's behalf.

"You know what, I think you might just be right," agreed Dad, at last giving in.

From that day on, the robin always had its own special place at Kate's window sill. And as for that determined squirrel, Dad made sure to stock up regularly on plenty of extra seed balls, so that nobody need ever go hungry that winter.

Snowman in a Sulk

*By Calista, Darcey, Janasi, Jessica, Louise, Maya,
Sumedha and Zaki*

"Snow!" cried Jamie jumping up and down at
the window in his pyjamas.

"What are you on about? It never snows in
London," scoffed his sister, Margo, from the top
bunk. "Get back to bed. It's too early."

"Yes it does! And it has! Come and look!" insisted
Jamie.

Margo slid down the rails of her bed and loped
over to the window to join her younger brother.
She gawped in amazement when she saw for herself
the scene in their back garden.

It looked like something out of a fairy tale.
Everything was covered in a blanket of brilliant
white - the trees, the rooftops, the hills in the park
beyond, everything.

Still in his pyjamas, Jamie dashed down the
stairs and straight out into the garden.

"What are you doing? Come back inside," ordered his bossy big sister.

"Why? It's Saturday. There's no school. Let's build a snowman," Jamie cheered, frolicking about in the snow, trying to catch the lacelike snowflakes on his tongue.

"Okay, but at least put your wellies and your coat on first," said Margo, hurrying out after him, with Yappy, their dog, scampering about at her heels - he wasn't going to miss out on all the excitement.

The children worked together to roll a ball of snow around the garden. It grew and grew until it came up to Margo's middle.

"Now for the head," said Margo, starting on another ball.

The children worked together, but Yappy wasn't so interested. He was far keener on digging. He'd dig at every opportunity and, with all that snow, it was like digger heaven to Yappy - a whole extra layer to nose-dive into. Yappy liked to bury everything, from his plastic ball, to his rubber bone, to Margo's hair clips - he even once buried the remote control for the TV. It took the family weeks to work out where it was. It was only when Mum went out to the compost heap and noticed a feint red light flashing amongst the potato peelings that they rediscovered it.

When the head was complete, they heaved it up on top of the body and danced around the snowman with glee.

"But what about his face? He looks a bit scary without one," remarked Jamie.

The two of them rushed around the garden and back into the house searching for all the items and accessories they'd need. Coal for the eyes and mouth, a multi-coloured woolly scarf and a most grand, black top hat to finish off the look. But there was one thing missing.

"I can't find a carrot for the nose anywhere," sighed Jamie.

"Me neither," groaned Margo.

"How about the compost heap?" suggested Jamie.

The two of them scrabbled around in the pile of old scraps at the back of the garden.

"Nope. No carrot here either, just this rotten old potato," said Margo holding up the knobbliest, bobbliest, old vegetable anyone had ever seen.

"It's got pointy roots sprouting out of it. That sort of makes it like a carrot, doesn't it?" said Jamie.

"Good thinking. We'll use that instead then," agreed Margo, attaching the finishing touch to the snowman's face.

"It's a masterpiece," marvelled Margo, standing back to admire their handiwork.

"Yes. I like it a lot," agreed Jamie.

They played in the snow all day until it was time for bed. That night, they snuzzled down in their bunks, their heads full of the day's excitement, until they drifted off to sleep.

THUMP!

Margo sat up in her bed.

THUMP!

Jamie was awoken by the noise too. "What was that?" he cried.

THUMP! It came again.

The children's attention was drawn to the window.

THUMP! A snowball splatted against the pane. Then another, and another.

The children dashed to the window and looked down to find their snowman in a fit of rage, stomping about the garden, his brow furrowed, hurling snowball after snowball directly at the children's bedroom.

"What's wrong with him?" wondered Margo.

"I don't like it," whispered Jamie.

"Don't be such a baby. Let's go down and see what the matter is."

The children raced downstairs, grabbed their coats and wellies and waded out into the garden. Yappy, also stirred by the commotion, came scampering after them.

The rampaging snowman continued to fire snowballs at the children, giving Margo a white beard and Jamie a fluffy hat.

"Stop!" cried Margo.

"Why should I?" fumed the snowman. "This is all your fault after all."

"What are you talking about? We didn't do anything?" retorted Margo, ducking another snowball.

"Then allow me to enlighten you. I'm most probably the finest snowman the world has ever seen," he began, strutting around the garden as if to prove it. "I have the grandest top hat, a luxury woollen scarf… and yet… and yet… you have the audacity to give me a potato for a nose!"

So *that* was his problem.

"What are we going to do?" panicked Jamie.

"Don't ask me. It was your idea to use the potato," snapped Margo.

"I didn't hear you disagreeing. You even called it a masterpiece," argued Jamie.

"Pah! Some masterpiece," sniffed the snowman.

"Ok, ok… we're sorry. Now let's have a think…" said Margo, "but if you could kindly stop hurling snowballs at us, that might be a start."

The snowman folded his arms and slumped down in a sulk.

Whilst the children thought and thought, Yappy was frantically digging. After some time, he scampered up to the children and began running around them in circles.

"Yap."

"Not now, Yappy," huffed Margo.

"Yap, yap."

"We're trying to think, Yappy," sighed Jamie.

"Yap!" he persisted.

"We said, not now!" scolded Margo.

Yappy gave up on the children and bounded over to the snowman instead. The excited pup dropped something in his frosty lap and wagged his tail.

"What have you got there, chap?" enquired the snowman.

The children dashed over to see what it was.

"Good boy, Yappy!" cried Margo. "You've found a carrot."

Indeed he had. For Yappy was a dog who buried everything, including carrots it seemed.

The snowman plucked the potato from his face, flung it back on the compost heap and replaced his nose with Yappy's carrot.

"That feels wonderful. I must now be the grandest snowman in all the world," he declared, parading around the garden with pride.

At last their snowman was complete. He was indeed the finest snowman the world had ever seen, and all thanks to Yappy.

Santa and the Pesky Pixie

By Ashpriya, Harjeet, Keyshia, Pavan and Sai

It was Christmas Eve and Santa was busy in his study, reading letters and checking over his naughty list.

"Oh dear, not again," he sighed to himself, "Lily Pixie's been up to her usual mischief. Will she never learn to be good?"

Little did he know, Lily Pixie had in fact, just snuck into his grotto and was about to commit her naughtiest crime of all. She tiptoed up to the door of his study. The key was there in the lock. It was all too easy. Lily Pixie locked Santa in, fast.

Santa turned quickly in his armchair and stared at the door. He ran up to it and shook the handle.

"Ho, no, no! What's going on?" he said, scratching his beard.

"Ha, ha, ha!" grinned Lily Pixie, "You're not going to be delivering presents to any goody-goody children this Christmas."

Santa recognised that mischievous voice, "Lily! Why would you do such an unkind thing?"

"That's what you get for giving me socks every year!" Lily Pixie replied.

"But you know the rules. That's what *you* get when you're on the naughty list," explained Santa.

"It's not fair. I'm *always* on the naughty list," said Lily Pixie folding her arms and stamping her foot.

"Well... how about trying to be good for a change, then?" advised Santa.

"I can't, it's too hard. I'm no good at being good," she sighed.

Santa knew that the only way to get out of this situation would be to persuade Lily Pixie to change. Otherwise no one would be getting any presents, not even socks. He had to talk her round.

"Have you ever tried?" he said softly.

"There's no point. Everyone knows I'm really naughty. Even you. Every time people see me coming, they run away and hide. Or worse, they just ignore me. No one's ever going to give me a chance," Lily Pixie sniffled.

Santa realised that Lily Pixie was crying. He knew that deep down she must have feelings. Everyone had some good in them really.

"How about *I* give you a chance?" suggested Santa.

"You? Why would you want to give me a chance when I've caused you the biggest trouble of all?" replied Lily Pixie.

"You could start by letting me out of here, couldn't you?" ventured Santa. "That would be a good deed, wouldn't it?"

"Hmmmm…" thought Lily Pixie.

"And then, perhaps you could be my helper tonight. You might even enjoy it," continued Santa.

"Really?" questioned Lily Pixie, still not completely convinced.

"You'll never know, unless you give it a try," coaxed Santa.

Much to Santa's relief, there came the sound of the key turning in the lock, followed by a gentle creak of the door. Lily Pixie anxiously popped her head through and tiptoed into Santa's study. She stood there quietly, looking down at the floor.

"Now, now. Don't feel so bad. Everybody deserves a second chance. I'm grateful to you for unlocking the door. Well done, Lily."

Lily Pixie blushed. She felt strange. It was the first time anyone had ever said anything positive to her.

"Right then. Let's not dilly-dally. We've got work to do," smiled Santa springing into action.

He led Lily Pixie outside. There in the snow stood a great big barn. Santa opened the giant doors and inside was a hive of activity. Dozens of elves were busily preparing for the launch of the magical sleigh. They hauled hundreds of brightly coloured parcels over from the toy factory and loaded them into a giant sack. As the reindeer were harnessed to the sleigh, bells jingled merrily from their golden bridles. The sleigh itself was a magnificent example of engineering, made of the finest wood, and painted in red, green and silver, with gold streaks along the side. Elf mechanics made their final inspections, as more helpers heaved the sack onto the back of the sleigh.

Lily Pixie was amazed at the scene and couldn't believe that she was going to be part of something so special. But, believe it or not, Santa was already escorting her over to the sleigh and helping her up onto it. He climbed into the driver's seat and invited Lily Pixie to sit beside him.

Ahead of them, dozens of elves cleared a giant path through the snow. They strung hundreds of twinkling Christmas lights along it to create a runway. Santa took firm hold of the reins, the bells jingled and the reindeer pawed the ground eagerly with their hooves.

"Ho, ho, ho! Here we go!" cried Santa.

The sleigh shot forwards like a bolt of lightning. It tore up the runway and soared high into the air with an almighty whoooooosh!

"Wheeeeeeeeeeeeeeeeeee!" squealed Lily Pixie with delight, "This is fantaaaaaaaaaastic!"

High above the rooftops they flew.

Santa handed Lily Pixie a map, "This will be your responsibility," he said. "You'll need to navigate and let me know when to make a stop."

Lily Pixie felt very important and so proud. She studied the map carefully and located the first house.

"Two hundred metres north is where Jack lives," instructed Lily Pixie, "He's on the good list and has asked for a helicopter."

Santa steered the reindeer in the direction of Jack's house and landed on the roof. He collected Jack's toy from the sack and headed for the chimney, disappearing down it with a flash of magic dust. Seconds later, he reappeared wiping crumbs from his beard. He had a handful of carrots for the reindeer, and something else...

"Here, this is for you," said Santa, handing Lily Pixie a mince pie.

"For me?" Lily Pixie smiled.

"And you can feed the carrots to Rudolph and his pals if you like," he added.

"This is such fun!" cried Lily Pixie.

"See, I told you being good is not so bad," said Santa with another hearty, "Ho, ho, ho!"

Lily Pixie and Santa busily continued on their way, delivering presents across the land. Lily Pixie was certain Santa's tummy was growing rounder and rounder. It was getting to be more and more of a squeeze for him every time he emerged from a chimney. There were certainly plenty of mince pies to go around.

Lily Pixie proved herself to be excellent at navigating and reading lists.

"You really *are* clever," remarked Santa.

Lily Pixie blushed again. She was enjoying the praise. She thought, perhaps she might even get used to it.

At the end of a very long night, Santa slowed his sleigh and said, "There's just one more stop to make."

Lily Pixie looked over the map and the lists in confusion.

"But we've done them all," she said.

"Nope. There's definitely one more house to visit," said Santa with a twinkle in his eye.

"If you say so," replied Lily Pixie, still quite puzzled.

"And how about, as you have been so brilliant, you deliver this last one?" suggested Santa.

"Wooooooo hooooo! Do you really mean it?" cried Lily Pixie, "You really are super, Santa!" She threw her arms around him and gave him a big warm hug.

Now it was Santa's turn to blush with pride. They came to a stop on the final rooftop.

"This place looks a little familiar," mused Lily Pixie.

"Oh Lily, we've seen so many rooftops, they all start to look the same after a while," chuckled Santa.

All the same, Lily Pixie couldn't shake off the feeling that somehow she had been there before.

Santa handed her the most beautifully wrapped present of all. The paper dazzled with sparkly fairies and twinkling stars, and a picture of Santa and a special little helper shimmered amongst them.

"Go on then," encouraged Santa.

With a sprinkle of magic dust, Lily Pixie hopped down the chimney. She landed with a bump and looked around. That's when she realised the true magic of Christmas.

"Oh! Now I get it…" Lily Pixie realised she was back in her own home. "So this must mean, that this present is… is… for me!"

She gave the parcel a squeeze and tried to guess what was inside.

"It doesn't feel like socks," she thought.

She gave the present a shake.

"It doesn't *sound* like socks either."

She tore open the paper excitedly. She was so happy when she saw what it was. A cuddly Santa toy. It had a fluffy red and white hat, big black boots and shiny buttons down its red furry jacket. Lily Pixie hugged the toy Santa tightly to her chest and to her amazement, it spoke.

"Ho, ho, ho! Merry Christmas, Lily Pixie!"

"Wow! Cool! It even says my name. It must be when you press the buttons on the jacket."

Lily Pixie pressed another button and to her surprise the toy Santa began to dance and sing.

Jingle bells, jingle bells
Jingle all the way
Oh what fun it is to ride
On Santa's open sleigh!

Jingle bells, jingle bells
Jingle all the way
Oh what fun it is to ride
On Santa's open sleigh!

Lily Pixie clapped her hands and danced along with her toy Santa, for this was her first proper Christmas. The first one when she had actually behaved well. Santa was right. Being good wasn't so bad at all.

The Unexpected Guest

By Mattheus Daly

On the banks of Loch Swilly, on a beautiful grassy patch of land, amidst a cluster of fir trees, stood a magnificent country mansion.

Inside, the grand family of the Duke and Duchess of Rathmullen were getting ready for a special New Year's banquet which they were hosting for their impressive friends.

A polished, oak table stood beneath an ornate chandelier of the finest gold, with a hundred candles warmly illuminating the room. Thirteen places were set at this table - thirteen plates of the finest china, thirteen crystal goblets, thirteen sets of solid, silver cutlery and thirteen cotton napkins, trimmed with lace and embossed with the Rathmullen family emblem. Thirteen oak chairs, upholstered in plush, claret velvet, positioned around the table, waited to be filled.

The guests arrived in their gowns and cloaks,

trilling and chortling as they took their seats. Baron
and Baroness Dalaigh, who were never the easiest
to impress, swept into the room, their noses high.
Earl McSweeney entered, ordered a hearty glass
of ale and settled himself at the table. Lord and
Lady O'Neill arrived and sat beside the Earl, Lady

O'Neill entertaining him with her recounts of the latest family sagas. The remaining guests too were seated. The hosts joined them at the table. Twelve places were occupied.

Yet, there was an empty place at the table that remained unfilled.

"My dear, are we expecting anyone else?" enquired the Duchess of her husband.

"I do believe all are present and correct. Everyone is accounted for," clarified the Duke.

"How very peculiar. The servants seem to have laid a thirteenth setting," remarked Baroness Dalaigh. "Whoever might it be for?"

The hosts and the guests turned their gaze to the windows to see if there was indeed anyone else to come.

A mysterious mist arose from Loch Swilly. It swelled over the beach and across the plains. A shadowy figure emerged from the haze, silhouetted against the moonlight. He paced slowly towards Rathmullen House, between the fir trees, across the lawn, along the gravelly path and up to the bay window that looked upon the dining room, through which the partygoers gawped.

The unexpected guest glided through the walls, floated into the room and settled down at the thirteenth place at the grand, oak table.

He acknowledged a heavily framed, dark, oil portrait which hung on the wall above the fireplace. It was he in the portrait. And he was the aged Duke of Rathmullen, great great ancestor of the hosts themselves.

There were gasps. There were shrieks. Lady O'Neill even fainted. The entire party evacuated in fear.

The aged Duke of Rathmullen gazed forlornly at the table. All he'd wanted was to return home for a special meal and see in the new year with his family.

Yet now, twelve places at the table stood empty, with just one place occupied, by the ever lonely ghost of the former Duke of Rathmullen.

Cold on the Outside, Warm on the Inside

By Alexia, Anusha, Mahad and Simran

High in the night's sky, at an altitude of 39,000 feet, a Jumbo JM776 flew smoothly across the North Atlantic Ocean. Inside that plane were passengers young and old, those travelling with their families, others on business; some were worried, others, less so. By far the most anxious person on board was a nine-year-old boy named Mikael. As the engines whined on, he worried that the plane might crash, but most of all, he worried about his new life in England.

Not only was this to be his first time in London, it was his first time ever abroad. He'd not even left his hometown before, never mind Jamaica itself. His Mama had tried to reassure him, reminding him that Papa's new job in London was not only a great opportunity for his father, but that it would lead to a much better life for them all. Mikael was far from

convinced. All he understood was that England was a cold, grey place and he didn't want to move there. But of course, he had no choice.

The next morning, Mikael lay wide awake in his new bed, in his new house (he could not bring himself to call it home) with thoughts of dread bombarding his mind.

"If I hide from the day, maybe it will go away," he wished to himself.

His Mama soon put an end to that as she burst into the room, opening the curtains with a flourish and bringing him back to reality. He could already feel the crackling cold of the frosty outdoors, threatening to invade his world.

"Wakey, wakey!" she chimed. "Ready for your first day at your brand new school? Who'd have thought it, my boy getting a first class London education."

Mikael was reluctant to leave his warm, cosy bed, but his Mama whipped off the covers, forcing him to get up. Stepping onto the cold floor, standing there in his cold room, he instantly broke out in goosebumps and his teeth began to chatter uncontrollably.

"What's the matter with you, child?" frowned Mama. "Today is a great day," she said with pride.

"What's so great about it? I hate this day! And I hate England!" Mikael yelled, before bursting into tears.

"Stop showin' tantrum and get yourself ready for school, now," ordered Mama, thrusting Mikael's new uniform at him before heading back downstairs and leaving him to it. Mama had no time for fuss and nonsense.

On arriving at school, Mikael continued to suffer the coldness of winter. But the teacher greeted him with a warm smile and presented him to the class without making too big a deal of his arrival, which he was thankful for, at least.

"How about you sit over there, next to Ava? She'll be your buddy for now."

Ava pulled out the seat beside hers for Mikael and grinned. There was a twinkle in her eye and he instantly liked her. The best thing about her was that she didn't ask him lots of nosy questions. In fact, the first thing she said to him was,

"Hey, do you want to hear a joke?"

"Ok," replied Mikael with a shrug.

"Why did the chicken cross the road?"

"I don't know, why did the chicken cross the road?"

"The chicken crossed the road, because she wanted to get to the other side of the road," laughed Ava, seemingly extremely pleased with herself and almost falling off her chair in the process.

Even if the joke wasn't all that funny, Ava certainly was, and straight away, Mikael felt better. He had made a friend already. Perhaps things might not be so bad.

Before long, it was break time, although in Mikael's case it might as well have been called 'torture time'. As everyone lined up to go out, he found he was filled with anxiety once more. His heart thumped like mad. What if he froze to death out there? Again, he began to cry. He backed away from the door and huddled against the wall, hugging himself and sobbing with misery.

"What's the matter, Mikael?" Ava asked.

"It's too cold! I don't wanna go outside!" he protested.

"Don't worry. I can get you a spare jumper from the lost property box," she said, leading him by the hand towards the welfare room where there was a giant plastic crate piled up with all sorts of clothes, abandoned, discarded, forgotten.

Ava rummaged about and pulled out a large sweatshirt. "See, here's one you can have." Then she pulled out another. "How about you put two jumpers on, to be on the safe side? And here… there's a hat and this enormous, woolly scarf too… and some spare gloves… and what about this extra coat?"

Ava helped Mikael on with everything. It felt good, knowing that he had such a kind buddy to care for him.

"Thanks, Ava," he said, breathing a sigh of relief.

"Now, all you have to do is go and wash your face, then you'll be as good as new. That's what my mum always says anyway."

When Mikael went to the bathroom and ran the cold tap, he looked into the mirror and saw the funny side of things. He might have been a clown with all those extra layers and that giant scarf.

Feeling so much more positive, together with Ava, Mikael braved the playground, to cheerful cries of, "Come on, Mikael!" and, "Play with us!"

There was just enough of break time left for a few rounds of Monster Tag. Mikael got so hot from all the running about that he ended up taking off all the extra layers, including the gloves, and especially the scarf.

And later, when he got home and Mum asked him, "How was school, Mikael?" He found himself saying, "Do you know what, Mama? It was the best day ever!"

School of Ski

By Hasnain Alibhai

One regular February half term, a group of students from Westwood High School were off on their annual ski trip to Andorra, in the Pyrenees. As the coach spiraled through the picturesque, snowcapped mountains, the students indulged in the usual sociable activities that teenagers enjoy, listening to Spotify, Snapchatting and munching their way through endless bags of snacks.

"I've been skiing loads before. I hope they let me go on the black slopes," came a boastful voice from the back of the coach for the millionth time. That was Jeremy. He was such a know-it-all.

One of the boys, Josh, shrank in his seat. He'd never attempted any of the slopes before, never mind the black ones, whatever they might be.

"Are we nearly there yet? I can't wait to practice my Italian," piped up another boy, Ben.

"Andorra's nowhere near Italy. Don't you know anything?" scoffed Jeremy.

"Alright then, France then," shrugged Ben, flushing a little.

"It's not in France either. Or Spain, or anywhere. Andorra's its own country, you fool!"

Ben went as red as a tomato and pretended to be busy looking for something in his bag. The other children were relieved that Jeremy hadn't targeted them. Hardly any of *them* knew anything about skiing either.

Once the group arrived and settled into the hotel, it was time for the first day of ski school. At the resort, the ski instructor, who introduced himself as Filipe, lead the class onto the green slope, or as Jeremy called it, 'the baby slope', to learn some basic skills and play some fun games. Filipe spoke with a strong Spanish accent and kept calling Jeremy 'Heremy' which made everyone laugh. Everyone except Jeremy, that was.

"Right, team," he announced, having lined everyone up for a debrief at the end of the session. "You seem to be ready for ze red slope. Tomorrow we shall really enhance your skills."

The next day, Jeremy, being the annoyance of the group, decided to take a different ski lift while the rest of the class took the button lift to the red slope.

"Heremy! Heremy!" cried the outraged

instructor as Jeremy disappeared into the misty mountain top.

Jeremy soon learnt that he had taken the ski lift up to the off-piste black slope, which pleased him beyond measure.

"Well, well, well… look what we have here," he grinned, shuffling eagerly towards the start of the dangerous slope. Feeling daring, he launched off the bleach-white snow and sped down the bumpy, uneven off-piste track. Jeremy was attempting to 'get some air', as if he had a point to prove, when he encountered a rather large mound of rock-solid snow. He hunkered down into the race position, closed the gap between his bouncing skis and prepared to rocket himself into the sky.

"This should be a piece of cake. Easy as pie," he bragged to himself.

Jeremy reached the boulder of snow and shot off from it in a cloud of icy powder. However, the bumpy terrain had rendered his skis unstable and when he jumped, the blades jarred against a smaller ball of snow, about the size of a large pebble. This caught Jeremy off guard, causing him to spin out of control. Smothered in snow, he flew ten feet through the air, like a baby pigeon failing catastrophically at its first flying lesson.

When Jeremy finally hit the ground, his left ski clipped off and skidded down the remainder of the slope and out of sight. His second ski dug into the soft snow whilst Jeremy carried on bouncing down the steep precipice, dragging the ski behind him. This definitely was not going to end well. When he at last came to a stop, he was left with an excruciating pain in his right knee and a mountain of embarrassment to go with it.

"Owwww!" howled Jeremy, clutching his injured knee.

His dreadful wailing caught the attention of two skiers who came gliding swiftly across the snow towards him. As they drove to a halt at his side, Jeremy got a fresh sprinkling of cold snow all over his head.

"Hola, Señor, what seems to be the matter?" asked the first skier who had a freshly trimmed moustache and bright, reflective sunglasses. He spoke in a Spanish accent, though seemed to have good command of the English language.

"I want my mummy!" cried Jeremy.

"Aye aye aye! Look at his knee!" exclaimed the second skier, who, unlike his friend, had clearly decided to keep a very messy beard and stick with the more traditional, humungous ski goggles. The first skier shifted his gaze to Jeremy's battered and bruised knee.

"Oh Dios mio!" he exclaimed, shaking his head. "What is your name, young boy?" he asked.

"Jeremy," he sobbed.

The first skier turned to his friend and said, "Ok, you go to the mountain rescue station. Tell them Heremy has hurt his knee. Rapido!"

The second skier sped down the beaten track - he clearly had much more skill than Jeremy.

In less than no time, the skier arrived at the first aid stop, which was by the entrance to the ski resort.

"Please, we need help. A boy is back there in trouble," spluttered the skier.

"What's happened to him?" asked the receptionist at the front desk.

"He has hurt his knee very badly, he has much pain," replied the skier, his heart beating heavily.

"What is his name? How old is he? Do you know where he's from?" questioned the lady, her eyes fixed on her monitor whilst speedily tapping away at the keyboard.

"I dunno. Maybe fourteen. English boy, I think. His name is Heremy," explained the skier, still gasping for breath.

"Oh these young, reckless kids, always getting into trouble," she frowned as she continued to tap away at her computer. "I do not have any records of a Heremy currently staying here."

"But he told me his name, Heremy," insisted the skier.

"Oh," chuckled the receptionist, as the realisation dawned on her, "You mean Jeremy with a J."

"Yes, is what I said," the skier confirmed.

"Ah yes, here he is, I do have a Jeremy from England. I'll send a snowmobile with a couple of first aiders and a stretcher right away. I'll get hold of his teacher too. He's been asking after him. Thanks for letting us know, you did a great job."

The skier removed his giant goggles and wiped his brow with relief.

In no time at all, Jeremy was transported down the mountain to safety. The snowmobile paraded him slowly through a congregation of skiers that had gathered to stare at the spectacle that was Jeremy, wrapped in foil, all red-faced, like a giant hot-dog, wriggling about on a bright yellow stretcher. His wailing and screeching could be heard even over the roar of the snowmobile's two-stroke gasoline engine.

An ambulance was waiting at reception, ready to take Jeremy to the local hospital. The teacher in charge, already unimpressed with Jeremy's performance, certainly did not appreciate having to complete the small mountain of paper work that went with the incident too.

"Please sign here," said the receptionist, handing over a stack of medical documents.

The school office back in West London would have to be contacted too, not to mention Jeremy's parents who also needed to be informed of the situation. No doubt they would not be particularly pleased to hear of all the havoc he had caused either.

Meanwhile, the paramedics performed an on-scene check-up and prescribed Jeremy with a sedative, which gave everyone a break from his tireless screaming, at least. Filipe, who was possibly the most unimpressed of all, excluded Jeremy from any remaining lessons, not that he would have been able to participate anyway.

To add to his nightmare, Jeremy's classmates began calling him 'Heremy'. On top of that, he'd never live down the fact that the whole group had heard him crying for his mummy; and everybody, especially Josh and Ben, would tease him for that and question his 'amazing' skiing skills for the rest of his school days.

Tracks

By Aaryan and Tejas

It was a joyous day. From a clear blue sky, the sun shone down on the snow-covered land, making it glitter and sparkle, and the air was pleasantly crisp. A group of boys, who were on a trek as part of the World's Bravest Children Award scheme, trudged through the fresh carpet of snow, leaving a trail of deep imprints behind them.

"Come on lads, keep up," the group leader called over his shoulder. At the back of the line, Andy and Chris kept lagging behind. They were so taken by the scenery that they couldn't help stopping to capture the moments - Chris, in fact, was a keen photographer and found the environment particularly inspirational. His dad had recently bought him a fantastic Canon Rebel T7i camera, with a whopping lens, the size of something out of a NASA observatory.

"This is exactly what I need for my GCSE coursework," enthused Chris. "Just take a look at that!"

Something had caught Chris' eye. It flitted amongst the trees that lined the track the group were meant to be following. It gazed back at them from between the frosty branches. Chris and Andy were captivated by the magnificent creature, with its dappled, russet fur, its powerful dark eyes, its stately majesty. It elegantly gambolled towards a pond. It gently lapped at the icy water. It was, of course, a deer.

Chris engrossed himself in taking snap after snap. The deer scampered deeper into the woods and the two boys followed, respectfully keeping their distance.

"She's a beauty, isn't she?" marvelled Andy.

"This has to get me an A★ back at school," said Chris with certainty.

"Talking of school, we'd better re-join the others," pointed out Andy.

However, when they turned back, they realised that the group had gone ahead without them. What was more, they realised they had gone way off track. Worse still, they realised they were…

Lost!

Andy tried to recall what Sir had said to do if anyone got separated from the group. He racked his brains, he thought long and hard. Chris, however, was more interested in checking through the photos he'd taken, seemingly delighted with himself.

"What are you doing, Chris?" scoffed Andy. "This is no time for pretty pictures."

Chris looked up apologetically, scratched his head and had a think too. And then it came to him, "Walkie-talkie, that's it. We just need to radio them with our walkie-talkie… Wait… did we bring our walkie-talkie with us?"

"I think so. Check your rucksack," replied Andy.

"What do you mean, check *my* rucksack? Check

your rucksack. You're the one who's meant to have it," said Chris.

"No I'm not. Sir gave it to you," insisted Andy.

"Never mind. Let's just both check," suggested Chris. With that, the two boys rummaged frantically through their bags.

Nothing.

They looked at one another in horror.

"What shall we do now?" fretted Andy.

Barely stopping to take a breath, they searched around for clues as to the way back. After what seemed like forever, Chris was struck with a thought. It seemed so obvious, he couldn't believe it had taken so long for it to dawn on him.

"All we have to do, is find our tracks and follow them back," explained Chris.

"Of course," agreed Andy, wiping his brow.

Soon the boys were tracing their footprints out of the dense woods and back into the open.

They followed the tracks which merged with those of the rest of the group.

"Yes, we're back on the main footpath," Chris called out over his shoulder to Andy.

Just as the boys were beginning to feel optimistic, the sky turned an ominous grey. Thick heavy clouds consumed what had been an expanse of bright blue. It could only mean one thing. A snowstorm was on its way.

Large flakes silently and swiftly tumbled down.

Gusts were in full swing. Panic crept in. What if they lost the trail? Would the tracks withstand the snowfall or would they soon be extinguished? What would Sir say when they got back? That was, if they even *made* it back.

They continued their trek, persevering against the icy blasts which hindered their every step. Yet they knew the impossibility of stopping to rest. They knew they somehow had to confront the danger. They knew they had no choice but to keep on going.

Eventually they spotted a light in the distance. Blurred by the fog and snowfall, but a light all the same. And what a welcome sight it was.

"It must be the camp," Andy exhaled with relief.

The tracks were diminished, but that didn't matter now. They had the warm glow of the cabin's lanterns to lead them back to camp.

Sir was waiting for them. How grateful they were to see his face, even if he might be cross with them for going off track. However, his expression only showed signs of his being pleased to see them safe and there was no indication of any anger.

"Thank goodness you're ok. I was just about to call the emergency services and place a missing person's report."

Even if he had been beside himself with worry, he didn't take it out on the boys. They had been through enough already. Sir took them over to recuperate on two comfy chairs by the fireplace, with warm blankets and mugs of hot chocolate. They sunk into the soft cushions and sipped on their comforting drinks, thankful to be safe and sound.

Avalanche!

*By Adeline, Alexia, Amira, Anisha, Athena, Cara,
Despina, Jessica and Parampreet*

CRACK! RIP! Amelia Snowheart looked up wondering where the noise had come from. She was halfway up Mount Everest with her fellow explorer Kate Scott and all had been well. Up until then.

There was another crack, followed by a rumble. The side of the mountain gave way. Huge slabs of packed snow tumbled and crashed downwards forming a giant dust cloud of brilliant white. It drove its way towards the explorers, gathering speed all the while. It groaned and grumbled like an angry giant charging down the mountainside, a ravenous cloud-beast, showing no mercy.

"Ruuuuuuuuuunnnnnn!" yelled Amelia. The two explorers tore down the mountainside, gasping and breathless, their only goal, survival. Kate lost her footing and went plummeting down the mountain. Amelia raced away from the path of the avalanche,

but she could no longer see Kate, and as the side of the mountain continued to give way, a wall of ice began to build between them.

And then everything stopped, almost as suddenly as it had begun. Silence now. Just the lonely cry of a hawk as it circled the blue sky above.

"Kate! Where are you?" Amelia's voice echoed.

"Over here," came Kate's faint reply.

They could just about hear one another, but the wall of snow that separated them was colossal.

"We need to find a way through, somehow. How about we both start digging and try to meet in the middle?" suggested Amelia.

Kate attempted to move, "Owwww!" she cried out in pain.

"What is it?" asked Amelia with concern.

"My ankle. I must have twisted it when I fell. And... Owwww my arm! I think it's broken," winced Kate.

"Don't worry. You just stay still. I'll dig for the both of us," determined Amelia.

Amelia ploughed through the great white wall. Her hands were stiff with cold, but she plunged into the snow and continued to relentlessly dig. It would be a struggle to get to the other side. It could take ages. To make matters worse, the tunnel kept caving in. Each time she thought she was making progress, it collapsed again. But she kept persevering. Amelia was not one to give up and her friend needed her.

"How are you doing back there?" Amelia called out to Kate.

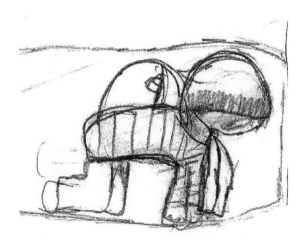

Kate was beginning to really feel the cold and was finding it increasingly difficult to keep up the brave act. All she could do was reply, "Trying my best, but be quick."

"Hold on, I'm coming," replied Amelia.

Kate lay on the frosty carpet shivering with cold, clinging to the hope that Amelia would eventually reach her.

Ignoring the pain in her frost-bitten fingers, Amelia battled on, clawing away at the endless snow, which ruthlessly gave way, again and again, from above.

Finally she was through!

She shuffled over to Kate and brushed the snow away from her friend's cheeks. Kate had gone blue with cold. She looked like an ice-statue. Kate's body temperature was dropping fast. Neither of the explorers wanted to say it out loud, but both of them knew that Kate was at risk of developing hypothermia. This was turning into a real medical emergency.

"We must try to keep you warm," urged Amelia. She flung her arms around Kate and held her close in an attempt to share her own body heat. But Amelia too, was beginning to freeze.

Neither of them would be able to get back to base camp in this state. They'd need to send up a flare. Thankfully, Amelia carried a flare gun, the silent kind that wouldn't disturb the avalanche any further.

She reached in her backpack for it. Her hands were so cold, she could barely press the trigger. Eventually, when she did, the flare just let out a measly spark, then fizzled to nothing.

"It won't ignite!" despaired Amelia.

"That's it. We'll never get home," whimpered Kate, so weak now, her voice was barely a whisper.

Amelia tossed her bag to shake out another flare. She struggled to re-load the gun and fumbled with the trigger. Her fingers were just too frozen. She threw the gun on the ground and stamped on it.

The flare shot up into the sky, like a rocket of hope. It exploded in the air with a bright crimson flame blazing boldly.

Kate and Amelia lay in the snow, gazing up at it. All they could do now was wait. And hope.

Apart from the occasional cry from the lone hawk as it circled the distant clouds, all was quiet, until... a rumbling noise broke the silence. Not another avalanche?! No... It seemed to be coming from the skies above, rather than the mountainside. Louder and louder, until a bright yellow helicopter was in sight. As it descended, the noise became deafening, the propellers beating so heavily that the snow whirled in great circles.

It was the mountain rescue team! They came dashing out of the helicopter, one by one, a parade of heroes in red helmets and reflective jackets.

The team wrapped the explorers in protective

thermal blankets and extra layers. They helped Amelia into a sort of chair-on-a-sledge contraption, strapped her in and transported her to the helicopter.

Moving Kate proved trickier due to her injuries. Working together as a team, they prepared to lift her onto a stretcher. Gently placing their palms under Kate's body - one took her head, two supported her sides, and another two held her legs.

"Ready… on three…" instructed the team leader, "One… two… three…"

And all at once, they raised Kate onto a stretcher. Kate grimaced with pain, but was too weak to cry out.

"It's alright," reassured one of the rescuers, she had rosy cheeks and a kind face. "You're safe with us now."

Kate, relieved at being rescued, closed her eyes and drifted into unconsciousness. She missed all that happened next. But Amelia didn't. From inside the helicopter she watched her friend slowly and steadily being lifted and carried over to the craft. Ropes and clips were fastened to the stretcher and with a clever array of pulleys and a lot of strength, the rescue team hauled it onto the helicopter.

The flight was amazing, with a mesmerising view of the peaks of Mount Everest. Yet, Amelia was more keen on keeping an eye on Kate. "Please be ok," she muttered.

Amelia and Kate were flown directly to the nearest hospital. They landed smoothly on the rooftop helipad and the two explorers were rushed inside to where they could be treated.

Amelia recovered fairly quickly. She just needed warming up and to be kept an eye on for a few hours, but after that she was discharged. As for Kate, it was touch and go for a few days. Because she had been lying in the snow for so long without moving, she really had frozen right through and she needed to go to the intensive care unit where a specialist team could look after her. There was a cast on her arm, and her leg too.

Eventually, Kate also pulled through, and she and Amelia were able to return to their normal everyday lives, although that life-threatening adventure was one extraordinary experience they'd never forget.

Scamps

By Abdifatah Farhan

There once lived a boy who loved adventures. His name was Arthur, so named after the great explorer, Arturo de Aventuro. One winter, he set off to explore the Rocky Mountains of Canada.

Halfway through an excursion across an icy valley, Arthur stopped for something to eat. He pulled out a peanut butter sandwich and just as he was about to take a bite, he noticed two unblinking eyes staring at his lunch. It was a bushy-tailed Arctic squirrel. Arthur offered it a nibble of his sandwich and found that the squirrel was incredibly tame. They instantly became friends.

"I think I'll call you Scamps," chuckled Arthur.

"How about you join my expedition?"

After gobbling up the last crumbs, the two companions set off again on their travels. As they wandered along the craggy mountain track, the sky darkened, the temperature dropped dramatically and snowflakes began to tumble down from the sky. Arthur shivered, Scamps shuddered. They would freeze to death out there.

Scamps scurried ahead in search of shelter. A crevice in the mountain led to a dark, stony cave. It would have to do. Shielding himself from the biting blizzard, Arthur followed Scamps in. But the entrance to the cave was lined with treacherous ice. In his keenness to get away from the storm, Arthur did not stop to take care. He immediately lost his footing and tumbled down a sheer slope.

Arthur somehow reached the bottom of the narrow tunnel alive, but it was only after the adrenaline-fuelled slide had ended, that the pain really kicked in. A searing, excruciating pain that raged through his ankle. There was no doubt, it was broken.

"Scamps!" Arthur's voice rattled through the cave. "I'm hurt. I can't get back up. You're my only hope."

Scamps dashed off to find help. He located the mountain rescue team in a hut beside an icy lake. How could he, a common squirrel, get their attention? And then it came to him. He knew exactly what he needed to do.

He went for it. Through the wooden door, past the stove, under the table, up the chair leg and onto a shelf, from which he launched himself onto one of the men. He snatched the radio from his belt.

"Hey! Stop that squirrel! He's stolen my walkie-talkie."

Scamps made a dash for the exit. The team gave chase all the way across the mountains, as Scamps led them to the cave where Arthur was still crying for help. His voice echoed up through the steep tunnel.

Arthur was hoisted to safety by the expert rescue team.

And all thanks to Scamps, the super squirrel.

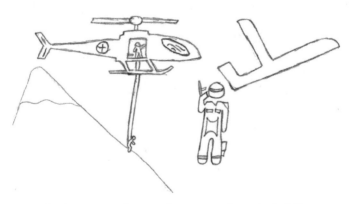

Arthur was taken to the nearest hospital. Of course, Arctic squirrels weren't allowed in, but Arthur made up his mind to go and seek Scamps out as soon as he recovered. He'd be sure to take his delicious peanut butter sandwiches along with him too.

Captain Cool and the Fire of Death

By Sam Beglin

Captain Cool lived in a submarine, deep in the coldest ocean. He was a very famous hero, with special super snow powers.

Whilst scanning the globe for world disasters, his radar alerted him to a problem. A baddie was causing chaos in Ireland. It was the Villainous Volcan, up to his usual mischief, and he had set the city of Dublin on fire.

Captain Cool blasted off to Ireland, tearing through the sea like a bullet. He reached Dublin and found the Villainous Volcan on the highest building, hurling fire-bolts everywhere.

Captain Cool climbed out of his submarine and flew up to the roof of City Hall. The Villainous Volcan had not noticed Captain Cool (even though he was really high up).

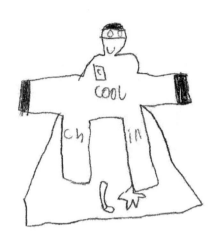

Captain Cool used his snow powers to quickly put out the flames, but just as he was about to deal with Volcan, he heard an almighty roar.

Volcan had created a fiery dragon that breathed out even greater fire-bolts than his master had thrown. The dragon tried to shoot Captain Cool but he was too quick for him.

Captain Cool could tell that he needed more power in order to defeat the dragon and Volcan, so he thought of an idea. He knew he could speak to the creatures of the deep and so he dove into the sea and summoned a giant whale and a swarm of swordfish.

Together they formed a water tornado. The dragon was scared of water and tried to fly away, but a jet spray struck its wing. The dragon lost control and came hurtling down. When it hit the ocean it fizzled away into the water.

splash

Volcan was horrified and also furious. He soared down in a rage, preparing to hurl more fire-bolts, but Captain Cool punched him, sending Volcan smashing backwards through the buildings. After all that, he had no power left so he ran away before the police could arrest him.

From that day on, the Villainous Volcan was never seen again. OR WAS HE? No he wasn't. As for Captain Cool… well, he flew back down to his submarine and returned to his home, deep in the coldest ocean, until it would be time to rise again.

The Ice Queen

By Daniela Burger

Frost had painted every inch of the orphanage's windows, and a thick carpet of snow covered the rooftops and surrounding fields. Crystal lay awake in her bed, shivering from head to toe, going over her escape plan in her mind. Tomorrow would be her tenth Christmas, and she didn't want to spend it in a cold, uncaring orphanage. She had never even set foot out of the grounds, but that night she'd decided things must change.

Crystal waited until she was sure that everyone was asleep, especially Mrs Swiffle, the mistress. She carefully stepped out of bed, and crept along the corridor and down the stairs, avoiding any creaky steps along the way. She cautiously made her way to the kitchen, the only place where the windows were kept open at night. She climbed onto the counter like a cat and jumped through the nearest window, out into the winter's night.

It was a good thing she had remembered to bring along her warm coat.

The stars shone brightly and the moon lit her way along the snow-covered fields. Venturing towards the empty road, she quickened her pace. Crystal rushed across the road, past an old farm and disappeared into a dense forest.

She came to a halt, breathing deeply. Luckily no one seemed to notice that she had escaped, so far.

Crystal, exhausted, curled up in a hollow tree trunk, which provided some shelter from the cold night air. She slept fitfully with the suspicious feeling that someone was watching her.

The next morning, she woke up, startled. This wasn't where she had run off to. The woods were more magical. The short, bulky oaks had transformed into tall pine trees and the wind whispered eerily through their branches. A ghostly mist hung in the air and that same sense of being watched remained ever present.

She slowly climbed out of the hollow and surveyed her surroundings with intrigue. In the

distance, stood a magnificent castle which certainly hadn't been there before. Despite the fact that she felt afraid, not to mention extremely confused, Crystal made her way towards the castle.

Fluffy, green moss crept up the cracked, stone walls, and the narrow, arched windows were invaded with cobwebs. A large wooden door, which Crystal assumed was the entrance, was slightly ajar, revealing a seemingly endless, dusty staircase. This place was certainly mysterious, and Crystal still continued to wonder how she had come to be there.

She gently pushed the door further open, and although expecting to feel warmth inside, she experienced a bitter chill instead. It was freezing. Pulling on her pink, furry hood, Crystal wandered up the icy steps, being careful not to slip.

After climbing for what seemed like forever, she was met with a scene that blew her mind. A massive hall, spacious enough to fit a dozen blue whales in. The air was filled with clouds of gem dust and the room shimmered with ice statues from top to bottom. It was packed with them. A narrow aisle down the centre was the only clearing. The statues were of all different shapes and sizes. Most of them were human, but Crystal also spotted a few dragons here and there, and occasionally she would slow down her pace to marvel at a unicorn with a long, flaxen mane.

A tear trickled down her cheek. They all looked so sorrowful. She was struck by a thought, a dark

thought that gave her the creeps. What if every ice statue in the hall, including the fantastical creatures, had once been alive? But who was behind all this? And why? Crystal's mind whirled.

Suddenly, from behind, there came the sound of loud footsteps approaching. She was frightened out of her very skin. Crystal turned in terror to see who it was – a muscular, giant of a man, dressed in dazzling, silver armour. He strode towards her wearing an angry expression which made him appear all the more brutal.

"What are you doing here?" he bellowed.

"Intruders are forbidden, Queen's orders! Who are you, anyway?"

"I…" she mustered up all the courage she could find, "I am Crystal Starika, and I need you to tell me who froze all these beings. They must be saved!"

"Or…?"

"Or, I…er…I'll…I'll destroy you!"

"Good luck with that," replied the guard sarcastically.

Crystal stepped up to him and kicked him hard on the leg.

He cried like a baby.

"Fine. I'll tell you, but keep it down. So, here we go… This castle is owned by the Ice Queen, who…"

"The Ice Queen? Oh, sorry, please go on…"

"…who happens to be the cruellest person of all time. She has a magic wand, you see, which she uses to freeze things…"

"Ok, thanks…" Crystal rushed past him, without further ado. She was compelled to find that wand. Somehow she felt it was her destiny to do so.

She hastily searched the castle, until she reached the tallest tower, from which a formidable female figure loomed, frightening the life out of Crystal.

She had wispy, white hair and wore a long, furry cape bejewelled with glittery snowflakes. Her narrow, blue eyes reflected the coldness of her heart. It was her. The Ice Queen.

"Who are you? Get out, now, before I freeze you
with my wand!" she commanded in a hoarse voice,
withdrawing a smooth, sharp, glass rod from her
gown, and pointing it directly at Crystal.

"My name is Crystal, and I won't let you get
away with this any longer," she declared in defiance.

Crystal snatched up the wand and raced down
the spiral staircase to the hall. But before she was
even half way down, someone grabbed her. It was
the guard again.

"Get off!" she screamed, struggling desperately to free herself from his strong grip.

"It's ok. I'm on your side. I've had enough of the Ice Queen and her evil ways. You're right. She needs to be stopped. I'm working for you now, if you'll have me that is…"

"But… but…" Crystal wasn't certain what to make of this sudden turn of events, yet there was no time to lose.

"Quick, follow me," signalled the guard, "I know a way out."

"But what about the others? All those poor frozen statues?" agonised Crystal.

"The answer's right there in your hands. You've got the Ice Queen's wand, haven't you? It is the source of all her powers."

At that moment, the Ice Queen came gliding after them.

"She can fly?" cried Crystal, aghast.

"She can do a lot of things," trembled the guard.

"Give me back my wand!" roared the fuming Ice Queen.

"Never!"

"Remember," prompted the guard, "it's the source of all her powers."

Crystal twisted the smooth wand around in the palm of her hand wistfully, "Then it must be destroyed!" she proclaimed. And with that, she hurled it down onto the stone steps where it shattered into a million frosty fragments.

"How dare you?" shrieked the Ice Queen. Her eyes went red, her skin cracked, her hair fell out. Then she exploded into a cloud of smoke, which floated off, through the arched windows, beyond the castle walls and far across the skies. That was the end of the Ice Queen.

"You did it!" cried the guard.

"Actually, *we* did it," Crystal hugged him.

"I'm Christoph, by the way," he said, at last having the opportunity to introduce himself properly.

"What about the ice statues?" remembered Crystal.

"Now that the wand's gone, they'll be back to normal, I should hope," replied Christoph.

They hurriedly made their way down to the hall. Christoph was right. The spell was indeed broken, just as the wand had been. The entire hall was filled with life. The clouds had lifted, the cold air was no more, and the room was flooded with rays of sunshine. Crystal immediately sought out the unicorn that had caught her attention earlier. It looked even more beautiful as it glowed with colour and happiness.

"He used to be mine," said Christoph unexpectedly, "I called him Dashmirror. I couldn't bear to watch when the Ice Queen froze him."

The unicorn trotted up to Christoph and nuzzled his master's big burly shoulder.

"Would you let me ride him?" asked Crystal.

"Of course," replied Christoph. "It's the least I can do. Where are you headed, anyway?"

Crystal hung her head, "I… I… I'm not so sure. I don't really have a home. I don't have any family to speak of."

"Well you do now, 'cos you've got Dashmirror here and me, haven't you?"

Crystal wiped a tear from her cheek and dove into Christoph's arms. He gave her the biggest and best fatherly bear hug ever. Dashmirror nickered softly. For the first time in her life, Crystal belonged.

Crystal climbed onto the unicorn's back and Christoph summoned another faithful guard horse. Leaving the castle and the ghostly memory of the Ice Queen behind them, together they galloped off into the enchanted forest ready to take on a world of new beginnings.

The Cold Situation

By Pavan, Sai, Keyshia, Harjeet and Ashpriya

Zillions of light-years away, in the depths of outer space, there existed a great planet. It was a sphere of the palest blue, encircled with white rings. It was the Cold Planet, so called because it was made entirely of ice and the temperature was always below zero. Yet life existed well on the Cold Planet as its citizens had adapted to the climate and their environment. They wore fur coats and had excellent technology in their homes. The Cold Planet was governed by King Frosticus and everyone lived happily under his rule as he was very wise and always fair.

King Frosticus had two children. They were twins, Snowdrop, a girl, and Snowball, a boy. Sadly their mother had died when they were infants, but King Frosticus had brought them up lovingly and they were all quite content.

However, things changed when King Frosticus grew older and eventually passed away. The time had come to choose a new ruler. But who should take the throne? That was when the twins began their quarrel.

"So, I suppose *I'll* be King now," declared Snowball.

"Says who?" retorted Snowdrop.

"Says *me*!" shouted Snowball.

"But why should *you* be King? I'm your twin, I have just as much right to the throne as you," argued Snowdrop.

"But I'm far more intelligent than you are. I'd be able to handle all the money matters and write up the laws of the land. You could never do that," disputed Snowball.

"That may well be so, but what about our culture and social morale? You are hopeless at sport and art, whereas I am the best ice-skater on the planet and everyone knows about my famous ice sculptures. Plus, I am the one who our subjects want to talk to, because you are such a hopeless listener," replied Snowdrop.

Both twins stood staring at one another and at the same time proclaimed, "This means war!"

It wasn't long before they had established two separate armies to fight it out. The battle took place at the Great Ice Pit in the middle of the Cold Planet. It was the worst war of all time.

Snowdrop appeared to be winning at first, using her powers to turn her enemies into ice statues. Her soldiers skated about, smashing them to pieces with their ice-clubs.

However, Snowball had a secret, powerful ally and the time had come to release him from the depths of the Great Ice Pit in which he dwelled.

"I call upon Big-Fist of the Ice Pit to show himself!" hollered Snowball.

The ground began to shake and crack. A giant muscular blue arm punched its way through the pit, followed by another. Sharp talons clawed their way up the ice. A fearsome head appeared with glaring eyes of orange and a shock of sharp, icicle spikes for hair; its ears were enormous and its teeth were jagged and broken. This was Big-Fist, the fiercest troll of the Cold Planet, and he belonged to Snowball.

Big-Fist bombarded Snowdrop's army with giant snowballs. He shook his hulking head and enormous shafts of ice, like spears, shot out and fired in all directions.

The battlefield was chaotic, with soldiers from both armies under attack and flying all over the place. Everything was such a blur. Nothing was being resolved. It was just a tragic scene of waste.

"STOP!" boomed a deep voice from the skies.

Everyone halted. Who had said that?

And then the voice came again.

"You've got this all wrong," it spoke.

Everyone gazed upwards. The mysterious voice seemed to be coming from the stars which then came together to form the face of King Frosticus himself.

Everyone dropped to their knees and bowed in respect.

"This fighting is pointless. You must think of a better solution," Frosticus insisted.

Everyone got to their feet and scratched their heads. They looked from one person to the next, hoping someone amongst them might have an idea.

It all seemed too impossible, until a tiny voice called out from the back of the crowd.

"Excuse me. May I make a suggestion?" came the little voice.

The crowds parted, and a small boy emerged from amongst them. Everyone gasped.

"You? How would such a pip-squeak of a boy as you know what to do?" sneered Snowball.

"You should learn to listen to people," Snowdrop reminded her brother.

"Snowdrop is right," came Frosticus' voice from the stars once more. "It should not matter how big or small anyone is. The tiniest of us can have the greatest of ideas."

"Those are wise words, Father," agreed Snowdrop.

"Let the boy speak then, since nobody else seems to have any suggestions," shrugged Snowball.

The little boy stepped forward and bowed. "Thank you, your majesties," he said. "What I wanted to say was, how about we take a vote? Whoever gets the most votes can be our new ruler."

The crowd rubbed their chins and murmured amongst themselves, making comments such as, "Hmmm, that's not a bad idea," and "wise words," or "that boy knows what he's talking about," and "ingenious plan!"

"That settles it then," confirmed Frosticus. "We shall put it to the vote. But before anyone decides, I call upon Prince Snowball and Princess Snowdrop to speak to the people and put their arguments forward."

Prince Snowball stepped up. He took his place on a tall platform of ice to address the people who listened eagerly before him.

"My most respected subjects, I urge you to choose me. As your new monarch, I shall manage money matters wisely and make all the best, most informed decisions regarding the laws of the land. Place your trust in me and I promise I shall not let you down."

The crowd clapped and cheered, they waved their hands in the air and roared their approval. As Snowball left the stage, he gave Snowdrop a smug look of superiority, "Try and beat that, Sis!"

Snowdrop confidently stepped up to the platform and cleared her throat ready for her great speech.

"My dear, beloved subjects. My brother may have intelligence, but *I* am the one who has the gift of sensitivity. *I* am the one who can listen to you and really understand your problems and needs. *I* am the one who truly cares."

The crowd were cheering already. This was a good speech. Snowball did not look quite so self-righteous now.

Snowdrop continued, "I can also promise that the culture of our nation will flourish. Sports and the Arts are my speciality and I shall ensure that each and every one of you has every opportunity you could possibly wish for. Place your trust in me and I shall take care of all your needs."

The crowd erupted once more. As Snowdrop left the stage she grinned at Snowball, "I think I might just have beaten that, Bro."

Frosticus spoke again, "Hush now, everyone," he said, calming the crowd. "It is time to cast your votes. I call upon Snowdrop and Snowball to take the stage once more."

The twins stepped back up to the ice platform, Snowball on the left, and Snowdrop on the right.

"Now then," spoke Frosticus. "All those in favour of Snowball, line up on the left and all those in favour of Snowdrop, line up on the right."

The crowd began to shift and stir. Some rushed to take their places straight away, whilst others dithered around in the middle, wondering which side to choose. Eventually, everyone made their decisions and two perfect lines stood before the Prince and Princess.

"I call upon the boy who suggested the vote in the first place, to count up the number of citizens on each side," declared Frosticus.

The crowd stood quietly as the boy travelled all the way up the line on the left hand side.

"How many votes in favour of Snowball?" asked Frosticus.

"Nine hundred and eighty two," announced the boy.

The crowd applauded, then fell silent again as the boy began to count the line on the right. Who would it be?

"How many votes in favour of Snowdrop?" asked Frosticus.

"Nine hundred and eighty one," declared the boy.

There was an uproar. Everyone on Snowball's side cheered and celebrated, whilst those on Snowdrop's side stood in misery. Some cried, "Booo!" whilst others demanded a recount.

"Silence!" boomed Frosticus.

Everyone hung their heads and shuffled their feet.

"The young boy has forgotten to count himself," explained the old king.

All eyes were on the boy. His vote was crucial. Who would he choose?

"I… I… I choose Snowdrop," said the boy.

Everybody gasped.

"But that would mean it's a draw," protested Snowball.

"There's only one thing for it," concluded Frosticus. "The Kingdom of Cold Planet shall have two monarchs."

"You mean, share the responsibility?" verified Snowdrop. "Of course. Why didn't we didn't think of that?"

The two twins shook hands. Both agreed it was

the perfect solution. They returned to the palace where there was to be a grand ceremony. Two splendid ice thrones, bejewelled with sapphires and diamonds were positioned at the top of the great hall. A glorious coronation took place, followed by the most excellent banquet.

What's more, Snowdrop and Snowball went down in history as two of the best monarchs the kingdom had ever known.

The Freezing Freakout

By Darcey McKeever
with additional ideas from Sumedha Hazari
and our Tuesday Creative Writing Group buddies

In a quaint village, high in the mountains, there lived a very merry family called the Whites. One snowy winter's day, Mr and Mrs White allowed their children Holly, Lucy-Anne and Peter to go and play in the woods.

"Hurry up, slow coaches," Holly called back to her brother and sister.

The three children skipped up to the woods. The scene looked like something from a Christmas card, with glittering pine trees and bushes like iced cakes.

"Yippee!" squealed Lucy-Anne. "There's snow, tons of brilliant snow."

The children raced into the wintry paradise and frolicked around playfully. After that, they wanted to explore the woods further. On they trudged,

deeper and deeper, until they met a fork in the path. They decided to take a left and found themselves following a strange, winding trail.

"I'm not sure we've been here before," hesitated Peter.

"Oh, don't worry about that, where's your sense of adventure?" replied Holly.

"As long as we're able to find our way back…" cautioned Lucy-Anne.

However, as they wandered on, they met a fierce snowstorm - a violent tyrant of raging wind and spiralling snow. It was as if the heavens had opened and decided to hurl the entire contents of its clouds at them.

"I'm scared," whimpered Lucy-Anne.

Holly shouted over the howling storm, "Quickly, everyone get into this willow tree."

They scarpered from the blizzard, into the hollow of a nearby tree. It was dank and gloomy inside, but at least it provided some shelter.

"It's dark in here," whispered Lucy-Anne.

"Ouch! What was that?" cried Peter.

"What was what?" stammered Lucy-Anne.

"There's something in here, it's sharp and it's spiky. I think it's a giant snowflake!" he exclaimed.

"Don't be ridiculous," retorted Holly. Although, immediately after dismissing him, she realised that she also could feel it too.

Lucy-Anne reached out into the darkness to find that there was indeed something tremendously icy taking up most of the space inside the willow.

The giant snowflake began to glow and grow, and from it a snowy white lady, holding a staff of ice, appeared.

"Hello," rang out the lady's voice, "are you stuck in this snowstorm?"

Peter replied, "Yes we are. Who are you?"

The mysterious lady introduced herself, "I am the Snow Queen. These woods are my realm."

"Then will you help us?" asked Holly excitedly.

"I will," offered the Snow Queen, "under one condition, that you will be my friends."

"Don't you have any friends?" asked Holly.

"I lost mine a few years ago," whispered the Snow Queen.

"But… how…?" faltered Lucy-Anne, worried that perhaps there might be something dubious about this strange lady.

The Snow Queen exhaled deeply and began her story, "I used to have friends. Very dear friends, in fact. They were the Sun Queen, Rain Queen and Cloud Queen.

"One fine day, we happened to be having a little fun, practicing throwing our power beams at the trees. The trees reacted immediately. Mine, of course, turned white as snow, Sun Queen's went buttercup yellow and Rain Queen watered her trees so that they flourished with vibrant leaves of green.

"But then, I accidentally threw a misguided beam which landed in Rain Queen's face. Another ended up on Cloud Queen's fluffy head and a third became tangled up in Sun Queen's rays. It was only then that I realised my silly mistake.

"But they were furious with me. They said I'd disrespected my own friends and that I had to 'face the music'. They shrouded me in a cloak of mist, bid me farewell and vanished. I've not seen them since.

"I am trapped in a permanent snowstorm. I never see the sun blazing in a blue sky, or wispy clouds floating by, or feel the refreshing rain on my skin. It's ever so lonely.

"Of course, I am too old for tears, but I am

deeply disheartened. I hadn't meant to do anything nasty. I was only experimenting with my beam sparkles, just as they had been. It was an accident. Truly it was."

The Snow Queen looked deeply forlorn as she finished recounting her tale.

"But we love the snow," reassured Holly.

"So, of course we'll be your friends," agreed Peter.

"Just, please, can you help us find our way out of these woods so we can get back home?" implored Lucy-Anne.

"I'd be glad to," replied the Snow Queen, looking so much brighter already.

True to her word, the children were whisked back to their village. Holly, Lucy-Anne and Peter kept their promise to the Snow Queen too, visiting her often, and they all lived happily as friends, forever after.

The Rainbow Tree

By Adeline, Athena, Cara, and Despina

What's happened? Where's the snow this year? Carol wondered as she gazed through the window at the lifeless sky. There was always snow. That's what made Christmas, Christmas. But not this year. Something wasn't right.

At least there was still the Rainbow Tree, she thought. Every Christmas, when Carol's family pulled out the tree from the dusty old attic, it was a different colour. It was quite a mystery. Some people believed that a tiny fairy lived inside the tree and changed it with her magic. It was as good an explanation as any for such an extraordinary tree, and Carol and her family had stopped questioning it. They just chose to enjoy the miracle of the Rainbow Tree and every year they went to the attic in eager anticipation, wondering what shade it might be.

This time, Carol went up to the attic alone. She wanted to see the tree first, without the others, as she still had a bad feeling about things. Her worst fears were realised when she climbed into the attic and clapped eyes on the tree. Her jaw dropped. Christmas was definitely ruined. The tree was black. Completely and utterly black. As black as coal. What was going on?

Carol sadly wandered over to the tree and reached out to gently touch its brittle, black branches. As she did so, she noticed her arm was covered in goosebumps. Her body tingled all over, her head spun and to her surprise, Carol found herself shrinking until she was the size of a speck of dust. The crumbs on the floorboards towered like giant boulders around her. She looked upwards into a canopy of black needles. She was underneath the doomed Rainbow Tree.

Then came the sound of giggling and whispering. Nasty voices saying things like, "That stupid fairy will never be free," and "Christmas is ruined forever! Ha! Ha! Ha!"

Carol turned to find a group of goblins rolling around in hysterics in the pot at the base of the tree. She marched over and stood boldly before them. They stopped when they noticed her.

"What are you all laughing at?" asked Carol.

"What are *you* doing *here,* you nosy little girl?" the head goblin challenged her. His name was Drujian and he was chubby with blue hair. He and his fellow goblins all had dark green skin and yellow eyes. They wore purple robes with green and yellow stripy leggings and big, black, stompy boots.

"You tell *me*, I have absolutely no idea," said Carol in confusion. "I just touched the tree and shrank and I ended up here."

"We'll have to tell her, won't we?" sniggered a skinny little goblin.

"So, basically," began the head goblin, "there's a fairy who changes the colour of your Christmas tree every year…"

"So the legend really is true…" marvelled Carol.

"She's called Merry Mary…" added a green haired goblin with a pointy nose like a needle.

"Not so merry now though!" cackled the skinny one again. All the other goblins burst into fits once more.

"Will you please explain," demanded Carol in frustration.

"We clever little goblins have got your fairy friend. We've captured her because she chooses to change this tree to ridiculously cheerful shades of pink, orange, turquoise and other such silly colours," explained Drujian.

"We like black better," another goblin interjected.

"Black's best!" they all chorused.

"We've trapped her in the star at the top of the tree and there's only one way to set her free. You must journey to the top, completing a series of challenges in the baubles you come across along the way. But of course, we all know it's impossible," said Drujian.

Carol gazed up into the vastness of the tree. How would she even reach the first bauble? But as she examined the base of the trunk more closely, she noticed a series of tiny steps spiralling upwards. Carol took a deep breath, "Well, here goes…" and braved her way to the start of the long climb.

Carol ascended the steps until she reached the first bauble. "Wow!" she exclaimed. "It's so beautiful." It was indeed most magnificent - a red sphere, sparkling with glittery snowflakes. She pressed one of the snowflakes and a doorway opened.

Carol stepped inside. Overhead, hung a row of candy canes, set out like monkey bars. Beneath, lay a chocolate lake which boiled and bubbled like the lava of the hottest volcano. It gave off such a tremendous heat, beads of sweat formed on Carol's forehead.

Suddenly, a deep, boomy voice came out of nowhere. Carol looked around and noticed a loudspeaker dangling from a piece of tinsel.

"This is Drujian the head goblin. I see you have dared to enter the first bauble. Well then, here's the first challenge…"

All the other mean goblins giggled and sniggered in the background. The fearsome voice of the head goblin continued through the loudspeaker.

"You must find a way across the hot chocolate lake. If you succeed, you may collect one of the keys to the star at the top of the tree," explained Drujian.

"But you'll certainly fail," came the voice of another spiteful goblin.

"It's impossible!" laughed another, nastily.

This just made Carol all the more determined, "I'll show you," she muttered, clenching her fists. But when she looked up at the monkey bars and observed how far apart they were, and when she beheld the gloopy, chocolate lake with its bursting, boiling bubbles below, she was not so sure. She was very agile and good at gym, but this was certainly a challenge.

She closed her eyes and inhaled deeply. She reached out for the first bar and leapt up. She just managed to catch hold of it and all at once she began to feel more confident. In the background the goblins were willing her to fail. They chanted through the speaker, "Slip! Slide! Slip! Slide! You must fall! You must fail! You must fall! You must fail!"

Carol did her best to ignore them as she swung from one cane to the next. The platform at the other end was in sight. Just one more leap to go. But oh, what a leap it would have to be, for the gap between the last candy cane and the platform was enormous. She looked down. The bubbles ruptured and raged. Not a good idea to look down. She pulled herself together and summoned all the courage and strength she could muster.

She swung herself back and forth, back and forth, increasing the momentum as she went. With one massive last try, she flew through the air just making it to the edge of the platform. She clung to the ledge, hanging on in desperation. Don't look down, she reminded herself. With all her might, she heaved herself up and scrambled to safe ground. She had done it!

Carol could hear all the goblins wailing and groaning through the loudspeaker. It was her turn to grin now.

"Ha! Ha! I knew I'd show you! Now where's that key you mentioned earlier?" she demanded.

"Look up, it's hanging over your head," stated Drujian coolly.

Carol reached up and grasped the first key. It

was in the shape of a snowflake, just like the ones on the outside of the bauble.

"Don't look so pleased with yourself. You've still got the other challenges and I bet you won't pass those," grumbled the head goblin.

Carol knew he was just being sour, and with the snowflake key firmly in her hand, she stepped out of the bauble. She found herself back amongst the black pine needles of the unfortunate Rainbow Tree. She still had a lot of work to do.

Carol continued on her way up the spiralling steps wondering what the next bauble might be like. As she climbed upwards, she heard a whisper coming from behind the black branches.

"Psssst! Over here!"

Carol noticed one of those mischievous goblins hanging from the next bauble. It was the skinny one she'd encountered earlier at the base of the tree. Now, without her fellow goblins, she didn't appear so mean. She had a funny smile and was beckoning Carol towards her. The bauble she sat on was white and fluffy, like Santa's beard, and had the words, 'Ho! Ho! Ho!' emblazoned on it in red glitter. It was a welcome sight against those ugly black branches.

The goblin hopped down and held out a bony hand to Carol.

"Hi! I'm Jado, and I'm here to take you through the next challenge which is the Christmas Riddle Test. If you guess the riddles correctly, you will

126

acquire another key to the fairy's star cell. But you'll have to be quick, because Drujian is timing you. If you're too slow, it will be the star cell for you as well."

Carol gulped. These challenges certainly were daunting. But she was a brainbox at school. She could do it. Couldn't she?

Jado pushed open the door to the 'Ho! Ho! Ho!' bauble and led Carol inside. The other goblins jeered over the loudspeaker once more, calling out words of discouragement such as, "She'll never do it," and "Soon it'll be the star cell for her too," or "I bet she can't even get the first one right."

Then they began chanting again. "We know the answers, na, na, na-na, na! We know the answers, ha, ha, ha-ha, ha!"

"Will you please be quiet and let me concentrate!" Carol yelled up to the maddening goblins.

Surprised by her boldness, the goblins fell silent.

"Oooh, touchy!" whispered one.

"Excuse us, we were only saying…" protested another.

"Just let her get on with it," snapped Jado.

Jado opened a box and presented Carol with three Christmas crackers.

"Here, choose one and pull it with me," she said.

Carol selected a gold cracker and did as she was asked. BANG! Sparkles and a plastic spinning top burst out of it, along with a paper hat and a scroll containing the all-important first riddle.

Jado unravelled it and read out, "What do snowmen eat for breakfast?"

Carol thought hard. This was tricky. She took a guess.

"Errrrr…. Frosties?"

"Correct!" cheered Jado.

All the other goblins giggled over the loudspeaker. "Hee hee hee! That was a good one!"

Carol heaved a great sigh of relief.

Drujian's voice broke in. He sounded very angry, "What are you all laughing at? We want her to fail, don't we? And Jado, we'll have less of that cheering, thank you."

Jado rolled her eyes and held out the box with the other two crackers in it.

"Here, choose the next one," she instructed Carol.

This time, Carol picked up a shiny red cracker. She pulled it with Jado. BANG! Another shower of sparkles and toys. Jado plucked out the second scroll from the debris.

"Ok, here goes… riddle number two. Why does Rudolph do well in school?"

This one was more confusing than the last, "Errrrr… because he was taught by Reindeer Claus?"

The goblins all tittered. This time Drujian sounded much more cheerful, "Wrong!"

"You're allowed another go, though," said Jado.

"But she'll need to be quick. Time's ticking away," sneered Drujian.

"Tick, tock, tick, tock," chanted the annoying goblins.

Carol shivered at the thought of the dreaded star cell. She must not fail. She thought really hard until she had a sudden brainwave.

"Is it because he's very bright and he NOSE a lot?" she responded.

"Correct!" applauded Jado.

Carol hopped with delight.

Drujian was furious, "Jado! I thought I told you! Whose side are you on?"

"Sorry!" huffed Jado. "Ok, onto the last cracker."

The third and final one was green and glittery. BANG! It exploded with a shower of rainbow dust reminding Carol of the fairy at the top of the tree and of all the beautiful colours she had brought so loyally to it year after year. Carol just *had* to get that third riddle right.

"Now then…" announced Jado, unravelling the last scroll, "What do monkeys sing at Christmas time?"

"How am I supposed to know that? I'm not a monkey!" snorted Carol.

"Tee hee hee!" giggled those irritating goblins over the loudspeaker.

Carol thought really hard, "Umm… we wish you a banana Christmas?"

"Wrong," replied Jado.

The goblins squealed with delight.

Carol's heart beat so fast, she feared she might faint. Time was running out. The thought of that star cell filled her with dread. No time to dwell on that now though. She must think.

And then, it was as if a light switched on in her head, "I've got it! It's 'Jungle Bells, Jungle Bells'. I'm right, aren't I?" Carol leapt for joy.

The goblins instantly stopped their squealing and tee-hee-hee-ing.

Jado's eyes shone, though she was careful not to make a sound, for fear of angering Drujian.

He was furious anyway. All goblins were bad losers, and he was the sorest loser of all, "I suppose you're right," sighed Drujian. "You'd better give her the key then, Jado."

Jado scrabbled amongst the remains of the burst crackers. In the middle of all the plastic toys and scraps of shiny paper, glimmered a metallic key in the form of a tiny Christmas cracker. Carol picked it up, and clasping it proudly, skipped merrily out of the 'Ho! Ho! Ho!' bauble.

Drujian grumped over the loudspeaker as she went, "You've still got one more challenge left."

But Carol didn't care. She'd passed the first two, what was there to stop her from succeeding in the third?

Carol located the spiral staircase once again and

continued on her way. She hoped the last challenge would be a bit lighter as she was exhausted. After an age of climbing those endless steps, she realised she must be getting close to the top because the tree was less bushy and the branches were becoming shorter. And then, there it was, just ahead of her, the third bauble.

It was made of the richest gold, with silver bells engraved on it and dotted with the most stunning heart-shaped rubies. Carol felt impelled to touch one gemstone which glistened particularly brightly.

It must have been some sort of trigger because as she pressed it, a door sprung open to reveal the inside of the third and final bauble.

Carol stepped through and found herself in a room with walls of green and a black, shiny floor. It contained a great deal of furniture, including an enormous wooden table surrounded by stools, making the room feel cluttered and small. There was also a blazing fireplace so it was stiflingly hot in there.

As Carol took in her surroundings, a familiar voice boomed out from above.

"So, here we are again." It was, of course, Drujian. "Seems you have reached the final challenge. You have just one chance at this one though, you understand?" He went on to explain, "On the table before you, you will see three bells."

Carol was surprised to find that three gold bells had indeed appeared, as if by magic, on the long wooden table. Each one had a question mark on it.

"Underneath one of those bells is the key you seek," stated Drujian. "The key shall be revealed to you now."

To Carol's astonishment, the three gold bells levitated above the table. There stood the key, in the shape of a miniature bell, beneath the middle one.

"Pay close attention now," said Drujian as the three bells lowered themselves once again.

Carol tried her hardest to keep her eye on the

bell which covered the key as all three of them whirred around, swapping places at great speed.

All the while, those irksome goblins chanted over the loud speaker, "You must fail and go to jail! You must fail and go to jail!"

Carol shut out the voices and focused on the bells. Try as they may to put her off, she wouldn't let them.

All at once, the three bells stopped spinning and shifting and came to a sudden stop. The goblins' echoes faded. Hush fell. It was time for Carol to make up her mind.

Which bell to choose? She went for the one to her left, but just as she was about to touch it, the bell moved. It made Carol jump. Was it a sign? Perhaps she should try the middle one then? As she reached for it, the bell radiated a tremendous heat. Fearful of burning her fingers, she rested her hand on top of the third bell to her right instead. She closed her eyes. She picked up the bell. It tinkled merrily. She dared to look. And there it was, the golden key, in the shape of a tiny bell, glinting at her from the surface of the wooden table.

Yes! The third key was hers. The time had come to free the fairy and release the Rainbow Tree from the goblins' ghastly spell. Off to the star it was.

Carol hurriedly made her way to the exit. There was no time to lose. She scaled the final few branches and at last reached the tree's summit.

There at the top stood the star cell, holding Merry Mary captive. She looked so unhappy, trapped like a fly in a spider's web, frozen under the goblins' spell. Carol felt terribly sorry for her. How could those goblins be so cruel?

But all would soon be saved, for Carol had the three keys in her hand - the first, shaped as a snowflake, the second, a miniature Christmas cracker, the third, a tiny golden bell.

She approached the star and inspected it closely. There were three perfect keyholes, shaped exactly as the keys she held. A sort of jigsaw puzzle for her to complete. She slotted the snowflake key into the first space. The star glowed a little. Quickly, Carol

inserted the second key, and the star shone more brightly. Lastly, she fitted the bell-shaped key into position…

There was an explosion of rainbow dust and the fairy shot out of the top of the star with a flourish and a twirl. She smiled at Carol and waved her wand, showering the tree with glittering stars and more of the exquisite rainbow dust. With another whoosh of her wand, she wrote the words 'Thank You!' in glitter, through the air.

The tree transformed into every colour of the rainbow. It was as if all the tints and shades it had ever been, had come together in celebration of Merry Mary's release. Carol felt extremely proud. She had defeated the goblins, freed the fairy and restored the tree to glory. But then, she looked down and realised she still had a big problem. How was she to get back?

It was as if Merry Mary could read her mind. She swished her wand once again and Carol began to tingle all over. Before she knew it, she was standing on the floorboards of the attic, beside the Rainbow Tree, back to her normal size. Merry Mary gave her a little wave before tapping the trunk of the tree three times with her wand. A little door opened and the fairy disappeared inside.

Meanwhile, things at the foot of the tree were not going so well. The goblins were gawping up at the multi-coloured branches, screaming in horror.

Blinded by the brightness, they gradually melted away, from the very top of their spiky hair to the tips of their curly toes.

Carol loomed over Drujian, "Bad luck," she grinned. "I hope you have a nice time, wherever you're going, but you don't belong here."

The goblins vanished completely. Well, all but one of them. Standing by the pot at the bottom of the tree remained a skinny little goblin with a funny smile.

"Jado!" exclaimed Carol. "You're still here!"

"Thought I'd stick around. I've had enough of Drujian bossing me about. It was fun in the second bauble, cracking jokes and all. I might even get to like Christmas," she smiled.

With that, Jado scampered up the spiral staircase to reach the white, fluffy bauble, the one like Santa's beard, with 'Ho! Ho! Ho!' written all over it in red glitter. Bidding Carol farewell, with a firm salute, Jado stepped inside her new home.

Carol stood alone in the attic, admiring the tree. She glanced at her watch. That was funny. It was still the same time as when she had first gone up into the loft. Things really *were* magical at this time of year, she believed.

Turning her gaze to the window, her smile grew even bigger. It was snowing at last! Great, huge flakes, floated silently down. Carol's heart was filled with joy. This was going to be the best Christmas ever.

How the Future Got its Snow

By Adam, Adeline, Athena, Cara and Despina

It was an ordinary winter's evening, much like any other and Chloe was playing at the bottom of her garden catching snowflakes as they fell from her favourite willow tree. She gazed up at the dazzling, shimmery icy strands which hung from its weeping branches and smiled to herself. There was certainly something very special about that tree.

Leaning against its trunk, she noticed a faded icy rectangle etched into the bark. She hadn't seen that before. She traced it with her fingertips and the grooves around the edges deepened. She rubbed away at the face of the rectangle. Wait… Was that a handle? She scraped away the ice and moss to find that indeed it was. She tugged at it and a door sprung open. Chloe lost her footing and tumbled inside.

Chloe looked around in amazement. She found that the inside of the tree was nothing like what she might imagine it to be. No mossy walls, no muddy ground, no creepy crawlies running in and out of the nooks and crannies. Instead, there was a floor of pristine white tiles and the walls and the ceiling were made of steel. A gargantuan, hi-tech engine loomed over Chloe. There was a chair too, exactly the right size for a twelve-year-old girl like her, and so she took a seat. Looking closely at the machine, she noted the rows of tiny saffron buttons and a panel of numbers. "I wonder what these do," she thought as she touched one, ever so lightly.

Immediately a strange automated voice sounded from above, "Welcome to the Time-Travellator. Prepare to launch in ten seconds. Please mind the gap between the trunk and the capsule."

"What?" gasped Chloe. "I'm in a time machine! I didn't... I never... I don't want to go..." she stammered. Chloe liked adventures as much as any other twelve-year-old, but this was somewhat overwhelming.

She pressed the numbered buttons in a desperate attempt to deactivate the machine.

"The Year 2004," it announced.

"The year I was born," gasped Chloe, frantically typing away.

"The Year 2010," stated the machine next.

"My best Christmas ever," remembered Chloe, although there was no time to dwell on that, as she continued to tap at the numbers.

"You have chosen the future. Prepare to enter the Year 3000," declared the automated voice.

"No! I didn't ask for that," shouted Chloe, slamming all the buttons at once in an attempt to delete the notification.

But the machine began to shift and shudder regardless of her actions. Suddenly, the floor and walls broke away, to reveal a gaping void between the trunk and the capsule. The words, 'Fasten your seatbelt!' flashed on the screen and the automated voice continued, "Launching in... 5... 4... 3... 2... 1... lift off!"

Whoooooooooooooooooosh!

The capsule blasted out of the top of the tree and into the air, leaving a trail of smoke behind it. Chloe stared down through a small round window. Crowds rushed about in the streets below, waving their mobile phones, taking pictures and hopefully calling the police. The contraption flew higher until the people looked like ants. It zoomed past a flock of birds, then an aeroplane. It floated through clouds, higher and higher, until stars and planets whizzed by. She'd ascended into space!

Chloe gaped at the scene. This was not the sort of outer space where astronauts went. No, this was completely different. The sky was dotted with numbers - hundreds of different dates suspended in the air, going back to BC and all the way into the future.

"Where's the 21st Century?" wondered Chloe.

"In the Milky Way," responded the Time-Travellator.

"What?!" exclaimed Chloe.

"All the years dated BC are in the Malteser Galaxy. You will find the years from Zero AD up to the 15th Century in the Kit Kat Galaxy, then there's the Twix Galaxy, followed by the Milky Way. Every year beyond that falls under the Galaxy Galaxy, which is where we are headed," explained the voice of the Time-Travellator, as if it all made perfect sense.

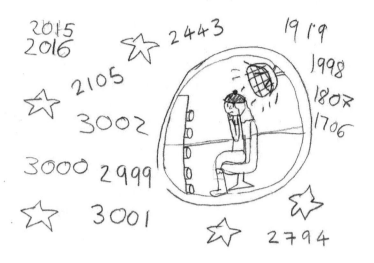

Chloe's mind raced almost as quickly as the capsule itself.

"Please press the gold button," instructed the automated voice.

Chloe did as she was told and soon the capsule sped up, faster and faster, until a purple, swirly portal, surrounded by stars, appeared before her. The capsule zoomed through.

Then, all of a sudden, the machine made an about-turn and began to descend. Back through space, down through the clouds, until it landed with a bump.

"You have now arrived in the Year 3000. Welcome to the South Pole. Enjoy your visit," announced the automated voice.

There was an almighty clang and a heavy, metal door flung open. As Chloe stepped out of the Time-Travellator, she was struck by a blast of icy air. Luckily she was still wearing her winter coat and her woolly hat and scarf from back home.

Bare, rocky mountains filled the landscape. As Chloe took in her surroundings, she noticed a group of suffering penguins. Strangely there was no snow. Just thin stretches of ice, and pools of still water which hung between the dips of the mountains. How could it be the South Pole without any snow? The penguins didn't seem at all healthy or happy. They waddled slowly and lifelessly. They wore a shock of gold at the top of their chests, yet their feathers were ruffled and they appeared to be sweating, as if full of some sort of fever.

Chloe stepped cautiously towards them to take a closer look. As she approached, the entire colony stood to attention and turned their heads in her direction. A hundred beady eyes scrutinised Chloe.

"It's ok, I'm not going to hurt you," she said gently. "I just wanted to ask, where's all the snow?"

The tiniest penguin of them all, shuffled up to her and offered her a wing. Chloe smiled and shook it. All the penguins clapped their wings together as if to greet her too.

The tiny penguin gave a little bow and spoke, "Hello, I'm Titch. You are most welcome here, but may we ask who you are?"

"I'm Chloe from the Year 2016. I was brought here by a time machine that was hidden in the tree at the bottom of my garden…"

"OOOooooh!" The crowd of penguins bowed together in awe and whispered things like, "She must be the one," and "She's here at last," or "So the prophesy really was true," and "It's a miracle!"

Titch patted Chloe with his wing. "Now, you save us," he said.

"What…? But… I'm not special. What do you mean, the chosen one?"

"You asked why there's no snow. Well here's why…" Titch began. "Back in the 21st Century where you've come from, humans have not taken enough care of the planet. Their wasteful ways have led to global warming…"

"I've heard a bit about that but I didn't think it mattered to me," replied Chloe.

"You mean, you've not been learning about it in school?" sighed Titch.

His fellow penguins all shook their heads in disappointment.

"Hang on a minute," said Chloe. "Are you talking about Walk to School Week and recycling and not chopping down the rainforests and all that?"

"Precisely. If you don't look after your planet, gases build in the atmosphere, causing the Earth to warm up. And as for the ozone layer… well, it's thinned to near non-existence. Because everyone has been so neglectful, we've had the warmest winters here and it never snows."

"But it's still quite chilly here in the South Pole," said Chloe.

"Quite chilly? Quite chilly is not enough for us penguins. If something isn't done soon we'll face extinction," warned Titch.

There was a sharp intake of breath amongst all the penguins, the babies began to cry and one of older ones even fainted - it lay flat on its back, its black webbed feet sticking up in the air.

Chloe scratched her chin and tried to think. These suffering penguins must be saved. But how? And then it came to her.

"I've got it!" exclaimed Chloe. "Back in 2016, where I come from, they're making the movie Mr Pingwin Goes to Town 3."

"So?" asked Titch.

"So, they need to make snow for the scenery. Tons of it," explained Chloe.

The penguin who had fainted, perked up at the sound of this, got back on his feet and flapped his wings. He was eager to hear more, as were the rest of the penguins.

"We can set the Time-Travellator for Hollywood 2016," Chloe continued, "sneak onto Mr Pingwin's film set, grab the snow blaster machine and bring it back here."

The penguins all nodded their heads.

"Cool!" said Titch. "Wait a minute though… what do you mean, 'we'?"

"You're coming too, of course," explained Chloe.

"I am? I mean… er… that's great… I think?" stammered Titch, who'd not even ventured further than the ice pond, never mind got into any Time-Travellator-whatsit to be blasted back to Hollywood of all places.

"Think of it as an opportunity," said Chloe.

"Hey, you're right," said Titch brightening up, "I might get to see my great, great, great grandfather. No… wait… my great, great, great, great grandfather. No… my father's grandpa and his grandpa before him, then his grandma's grandpa's…"

"Never mind all that," said Chloe shaking her head. "The point is, you will survive and you won't have to face extinction."

Every penguin gulped. They knew the danger they were in, but that word 'extinction' was difficult to take. Still, Chloe's idea did bring some hope and they all focused their unblinking eyes on her and listened on attentively.

"So, that's me and Titch. We just need one more volunteer to help us bring back the snow machine. Who's coming with us?" asked Chloe.

The crowd of penguins parted and a somewhat taller bird stepped forwards. He had crimson eyes and a cherry-coloured beak, and the most amazing yellow feathers which protruded from the sides of his face like a carnival headdress. His name was Punky and he was most keen to join the team.

"Excellent," grinned Chloe. "Now let's get going."

All the penguins gave Chloe, Titch and Punky a great send off, flapping their wings and dancing on the spot, as the three adventurers boarded the Time-Travellator.

Titch sat beside Chloe as co-pilot and Punky made himself comfortable in the back, plugging in a set of bright green headphones for entertainment. They strapped on their seatbelts and Chloe programmed the machine for 2016.

"You can press the gold button if you like, Titch," said Chloe.

Titch proudly did so and the machine began to vibrate as the engines whirred to life. The automated voice announced their departure, "Launching in... 5... 4... 3... 2... 1... lift off!"

Whoooooooooooooooosh!

It was another spectacular journey through space. Hundreds of digital dates flashed past, along with the stars. As the Time-Travellator approached the Year 2016, the contraption made its descent. Chloe's tummy lurched, in the same way as it might do when dropping down through a deep, cavernous elevator.

"You have now arrived in the Year 2016. Welcome to Hollywood. Enjoy your visit," announced the Time-Travellator.

Chloe's head spun. She was dizzy with exhaustion, but there was still so much to do. Titch was busily engaged in trying to get Punky to take off his headphones. Punky placed them around his neck and the tinny tune of *Mission Impossible* could be heard ringing through the earpieces.

The metal door flung open once again. Chloe and the two penguins poked their heads around it to assess the situation.

They had indeed landed just outside the film set for Mr Pingwin. Giant lights lit up a snowy, fibre-glass ski slope that ran through a replica townscape of New York's Fifth Avenue. Mr Pingwin himself was there, parading through the cardboard street as the director yelled instructions at the actors and technicians. In between film takes, a make-up artist ran on set to dab Mr Pingwin's beak with powder, causing him to sneeze. Another crew member dashed over and ruffled up his feathers with some sort of gel, making him look remarkably like Punky.

"Oh dear," sighed Chloe. "This is not going to be as easy as I'd thought."

"Why?" asked Titch.

"Look over there," she said, nodding in the direction of a security guard. "We need to get past him somehow."

"Not a problem at all," remarked Punky.

"What do you mean?" asked Titch.

"Well, we look pretty much like all the rest of the

cast don't we? Especially me, with my cool hairdo and all. I could easily be Mr Pingwin's brother," said Punky.

"Oh, I get it," said Titch. "We can just pretend we're part of the film."

"But I don't look like a penguin, do I?" sighed Chloe.

"Ah, but you could look like one of those special animal trainers over there, couldn't you?" suggested Punky, pointing a wing in the direction of a girl who was feeding fish to a group of young penguin actors.

"It might just work," smiled Chloe.

Chloe, Punky and Titch boldly strode up to the security guard on the front gate.

"Excuse me?" said Chloe. "I'm here with two of the cast. Could you let us through?"

"Pass please," said the guard.

"Yes, thank you, I do wish to pass, if you would be so kind," said Chloe stepping forwards.

"Pass please," repeated the guard.

"Yes, of course. If you could just raise the barrier for us, then we'll be on our way," insisted Chloe.

"PAAAAASSSSSS!" yelled the guard.

Chloe looked around and noticed that people in the queue were waving ID cards in the air impatiently. Then she understood. It was a security pass he was being so demanding about.

Chloe needed to think, fast. "Oh… er… I'm afraid this naughty penguin ate it," she said, frowning at Punky.

Punky put on his best guilty face and hung his head. Titch joined in on the act, shaking his head in disgust.

"What do you mean, he ate it?" scoffed the security guard.

"It… um… it fell on the floor and he thought it was a fish," stammered Chloe.

"But it doesn't look anything like a fish!" replied the guard in disbelief.

Chloe immediately signalled Punky to start choking. He made such a great drama of it, falling to the ground and clutching his throat. Titch had to try hard to contain his laughter.

"You see!" snapped Chloe. "You must let us through. He clearly needs to see the company vet. Urgently!"

"Very well then," muttered the security guard. "You can pass."

Chloe and the penguins made their way through to the film set.

"Phew, that was a close one," sighed Chloe with relief.

"You were brilliant, Punky," said Titch patting him on the back. "Perhaps you really should get a job here as one of the actors."

They crouched by the make-up trailer and surveyed the scene. There, right before their very wide eyes, stood the snow blaster. It was an impressive machine of white metal, powered by a noisy engine with an enormous, cylindrical canon and a giant propeller. As it whirred, it churned bucket-loads of soft white snow. It shot out flurry upon flurry, covering the film set in a glistening blanket.

"Wow! It's like magic!" whispered Titch in awe.

"What shall we do now?" asked Punky.

"Now, we wait," said Chloe.

"Cut!" shouted the director. The penguins toddled off to their dressing rooms, as the crew broke for lunch.

"This is our chance," Chloe nodded.

The three of them snuck up to the snow machine. They grabbed hold of the metal frame and heaved and pulled with all their might. Thankfully it was on wheels, but it was still extremely heavy.

"Not that way," whispered Chloe. The penguins were dragging the machine back the way they had originally come. "The security guard's still there. We'll never get past him with this great thing."

"How about over there?" suggested Punky, indicating a fire exit to the side of the studio.

They wheeled the machine around in the opposite direction and, as quickly as their strength would allow them to, they made a break for it.

But, as they burst through the giant fire doors, a piercing siren sounded, and red lights flashed all about the studio.

"We've triggered off the alarm!" yelled Punky in horror.

"Run!" squealed Titch.

"The Time-Travellator's not far, come on guys, we might just make it!" wheezed Chloe pushing the snow machine ever harder to build momentum.

"Stop! Thieves!" The security guard was hot on their heels.

As the machine gathered speed, Titch stumbled and fell flat on his face. He desperately clung to the machine, as it dragged him along behind it. His belly bumped up and down on the rough ground. Poor Titch.

"You won't get away with this!" The security guard was right behind them now, his eyes popping out of his skull, his face twitching and red with rage. Titch was almost in his grasp.

Chloe swung the machine around and pointed the canon in the security guard's direction. She switched it on and a jet of snow blasted the guard backwards. He flew several meters, his arms and legs flailing madly.

Titch picked himself up and the three of them made a final dash for the Time-Travellator, just in reach now. They clambered inside, hauling the snow machine in with them and slamming the metal door shut. They fell into their seats, panting breathlessly.

Chloe frantically pressed the buttons and programmed the Time-Travellator for the Year 3000.

Whoooooooooooooooosh!

The capsule flew higher and higher, leaving the Milky Way behind as it headed for the Galaxy Galaxy, far into the future where Titch and Punky belonged.

Titch hugged the snow blaster, whispering softly, "You're going to save our lives, you magic machine."

Eventually the Time-Travellator descended upon the Year 3000, in the South Pole.

The rest of the penguins had organised quite a welcome party for their return. They'd set up a red carpet and dusted it with the last remains of powdered ice. The baby penguins formed two lines, either side of the aisle, and sang in sweet, high voices, "Here comes the machine! Here comes the machine!" to the tune of 'Here comes the bride.'

Chloe, followed by Titch and Punky, stepped out onto the red carpet. There was a great cheer from the crowd. Titch signalled two of the strongest penguins to help tug the snow machine out of the Time-Travellator. As they rested it on the carpet, a hush fell across the crowd of penguins. They dropped to their tummies and bowed in respect.

Then, one of the little ones, who could contain his excitement no longer, ran up to the snow blaster, squeezed it and began covering it in tiny penguin pecks of affection.

"Stand back. It is time to launch the great snow blaster of the past," declared Titch.

Chloe grabbed the cable and plugged it into a socket on the side of the Time-Travellator.

"And now, the moment we have all been waiting for!" announced Punky.

Chloe switched on the snow machine. The engine whirred, the cylinder vibrated, the propellers spun. The penguins stepped back and huddled together, uncertain of this giant mechanical beast.

Then, right before their eyes, jets of glittery snow shot high into the air. The penguins squealed with joy and flapped about under a shower of crystals. Laughing away, Chloe skipped over to join them. She lay down on her back and moved her arms up and down to make a perfect snow angel.

"SNOWTIME!" pronounced Punky, unplugging his headphones and blaring music out of a loud speaker device he had concocted from the Time-Travellator. The penguins put on polka-dot party hats and danced away to Punky's tunes. "Funky! Funky!" they sang. Punky fluffed up his radiant feathers, rotated his head, jumped into the air, and landed with the splits.

There was a great big creamy celebration cake too, with figures of Chloe, Punky and Titch modelled in marzipan on the top. Chloe and the penguins had the time of their lives.

The Time-Travellator rumbled, its metal door swung back and forth as if summoning Chloe.

"Sorry everyone, I think it's time for me to go now," she murmured. Running over to hug Titch and Punky, her eyes filled with tears, "I'll miss you," she whispered.

A watery-eyed Titch handed Chloe a snowball and said, "This is my gift to you."

"But it will melt," Chloe replied, puzzled.

"When it melts, it will remind you of our plight. The snow blaster won't last forever," sighed Titch.

"I know. I should have listened more when my teacher was trying to tell us about global warming, then I might have done something to help stop it happening," agreed Chloe.

"Well, it's not too late," advised Titch. "There's still a chance. When you return home, you need to make sure that people do something about it."

"I will," she said, with determination.

As she returned to the capsule, the penguins called out to her, saying, "Come back soon," and, "You won't forget us, will you?" and, "Remember to save our planet."

Chloe stepped into the Time-Travellator and programmed it for 2016. The machine shook and shuddered into life then blazed off into the sky once more. Chloe looked down through the window and waved to the tiny penguins below.

When the Time-Travellator came to a stop, Chloe found herself back inside her favourite willow tree. The gap between the trunk and the platform sealed itself back together and Chloe stepped out through the rectangular opening in the tree and onto firm ground once more.

When she went indoors, she found her parents in the living room just as they usually were. It could have been any ordinary day. Dad was watching TV whilst Mum read the newspaper. Chloe was taken aback by the headline on the front page which announced in big, bold letters: 'MYSTERIOUS GIRL AND FISHY PENGUINS IN SNOW MACHINE SHOCK ROBBERY!'

Chloe smiled to herself. She went straight to the computer and sat down to design some leaflets for school about how to take care of the planet. Then, she wrote a very important letter.

Dear Prime Minister

I am writing to tell you that I am very concerned about Global Warming and that we need to do more to stop it.

If something is not done soon, temperatures will rise too much. Imagine the South Pole without snow, for example. It would probably be rocky with only a few patches of ice and slushy puddles. All of the penguins would get too hot and could even face extinction.

I have already designed a leaflet for my school. Could it be sent out to others too? Perhaps the government might also arrange for posters to be put up or adverts on TV to make more people understand as well.

I really hope you take notice of my concerns and help to do something about this very important matter. Our future depends on it.

Yours faithfully

Chloe Bond

PS. I wonder who the mysterious girl who stole that snow machine was.

"Let's hope that makes a difference," she thought out loud. And as she did so, she imagined somewhere, far away in the future, a colony of penguins, including a particularly titchy one, and another with punky yellow feathers and headphones, living happily together after, in a snow-covered South Pole.